I'M SORRY IF I SCARED YOU

MAE MURRAY

Copyright © 2024 by Mae Murray

All rights reserved.

No part of this book may be reproduced in any form or by any electronic or mechanical means, including information storage and retrieval systems, without written permission from the author, except for the use of brief quotations in a book review.

*To the queers of the American South.
No matter where you go, there you are.*

PROLOGUE

MONSTARA: Wakey wakey, eggs and bakey, Tennessee! This is Paranormal Mournings with your esteemed host Monstara on TVBN's 101.9 AM. The only Tennessee morning show unaffiliated with Jesus H. Christ.

(Canned Laughter)

The time now is 7 a.m. on November 21st, 2010. Today we're following up on a story that has rocked the Tennessee Valley since it was first reported to us on March 29th. For any new listeners out there, for our divine diviners and moonshiners, that night in March was a full moon. Our 24-hour hotline was ringing off the hook with reports of strange lights in the sky and unexplained gales sweeping the flatlands.

(Fade In... *X-Files* Theme)

Since that night, crop formations have been reported

across the American South at an alarming rate. Twenty-six have been identified and confirmed as genuine by the Mutual UFO Network, the Center for Extraterrestrial Language Studies, and British paranormal experts Rod and Maude McTavish, who went missing while documenting these phenomena earlier this year. This audio recording of the McTavishes was taken on the 26th of May and is the last known correspondence from the couple before they seemingly disappeared off the face of the earth. A warning to our viewers: What you're about to hear may disturb you.

(Soundbite)

(Wind blowing fiercely)

ROD: We're here in Wilcox County, Alabama, at the height of tornado season in Dixie Alley. As you can hear, we're experiencing gale-force winds as we seek to document a recent crop formation before it is destroyed by the storm. Maude is about 50 yards away, measuring the diameter of the smallest formation. We believe the pivot point—that is, the point at which this particular formation changes direction—is a signal to extraterrestrial aircraft, a map of sorts, to indicate the direction they'll be heading next. This pivot point indicates... Northwest.

MAUDE: [inaudible]

ROD: The wind is picking up now. It's impossible to

hear Maude. The weather is like a lion's roar in my ears, I can scarcely hear myself speak...

MAUDE: [frantic, inaudible]

ROD: [breathless] Maude has indicated a... Behind me, a large [inaudible] craft, just magnificent in... [gasp] in size. It's broad daylight, I've never... [inaudible] very bold alien contact... It feels as if I'm in a vacuum, in which gravity has ceased to exist. I can scarcely... [inaudible] oxygen has thinned and across the formation I can see that Maude's feet are no longer touching the... Maude! Maude!

MAUDE: [inaudible, screaming]

ROD: Maude, Darling! Darling... [weeping] We are both being held aloft directly below the craft. It appears as a... strange shape, like a clam's shell, the mouth of which is opening now to receive us. This may be my last [gasping] correspondence. My final act will be to throw this recording outside the range of the aircraft's magnetism. I do not know what awaits me inside the clamshell. There is a tongue, extending from the mouth. I feel... [inaudible, wind] my skin. I can't breathe. I love my wife.

(Wind whistling. Scratching. Silence.)

(End Soundbite)

MONSTARA: Rod's last act may have provided researchers with the most compelling evidence of extraterrestrial intelligence, and a description of alien aircraft that differs from what has been documented in the past. Since the McTavish Incident, crop formations have continued to appear, making 2010 the year with the most reported *by far*. Astrologers have speculated the increase in alien activity may be attributed to the upcoming lunar eclipse, which will occur on December 21st. It is the first total lunar eclipse to take place on the winter solstice since 1638.

(Ghostly groaning. Whistling wind. *Brrrrr.*)

We will continue to update this report as more of the story is made available to us. In the meantime, if you have any information on the disappearance of Rod and Maude McTavish, please contact our 24-hour hotline at [redacted]. This has been Monstara with Paranormal Mournings, where no incident is coincidence.

(End Broadcast)

PART 1
HELL IS REAL

1

SHE COULDN'T SAY her car ran well or that it would even get her from Massachusetts to Arkansas, but it was one of the few things that she could call *hers*, and she was bleeding on the cigarette-charred seat.

2

THE ABORTION PILL was working by the time Odette Tucker hit Connecticut, her stomach cramping and bloating against her waistline so she had to open her jeans. Entering Pennsylvania, she abandoned pants altogether. She sat on a towel folded into quarters and bunched under the stain in her panties, the scent of American soil wafting through the drafty vents of the broken AC.

The first time she rubbed herself against a bare cock with her pants around her ankles, she was with a college newspaper photographer. It was on a school trip to New York City, hidden away in a hotel closet. She had refused to go all the way out of mortal terror of pregnancy, had fled and left him hard in the cold room, a sizable pink dick shriveling at the rejection.

Later, she lost her virginity to the dean's son at a Halloween party, after they'd been making eyes all night. It was in a college-kid flophouse littered with stale popcorn and empty pizza boxes, smelling thickly of booze and body odor.

Her exaggerated moans were drowned by a beer pong competition in the next room. In the middle of fucking, she asked him why he liked her, and he said, "Because you have big titties." She realized, not for the first time in her life, that these things meant more to her than they did to someone else. She vowed to stop caring.

The dean's son had used a condom. After that sorry sexual awakening, she tried birth control for a while, but it just made her crazy, crazy and sad and unable to control all that crazy and sad, unable to contain it as a woman should.

So she had stopped birth control, and some time later she was raped. It was a rite of passage. She was raped as her mother was raped and as her grandmothers before her were raped—before they really called it rape —the violence rippling on and on forever, past and future muddled in a mixing bowl.

Now she sped down the great American highway, on her way home for Thanksgiving, aborting the clump of cells that would have been a baby someday if she let it.

3

SHE STOPPED TWICE IN PENNSYLVANIA, once in Maryland, and once in each of the Virginias, but the not-baby would not come. She bore herself over roadside toilets, changing out bloody pads and aching, pushing as if she were in genuine labor, and found the thing *still* would not come.

Over the days, she developed a necessary affection for the pain, sweating and singing to too-loud music to drown the urgency of the cramps at the base of her stomach, cursing and praying for the not-baby in equal measure, and still the damned thing *would not come!*

And then she hit Tennessee.

4

AFTER THE RAPE, she wanted to call Momma. It felt strange to long for her, a primal pull toward a mother she had never really known and who had never really known her. This feeling had been tamped down by necessity over years and years of absence; in and out of jail and rehabs, falling off the edge of the earth for long stretches of time, living rough under an overpass, Odie once heard, or operating an illegal beagle mill where all the pups sickened and died of parvo.

She wasn't sure if she had her mother's most recent number, her phones paid for by the text or minute and always on rotation. Momma could go a year or more without a phone. Calling her, Odie never knew if she would get Momma or some stranger, and often there was little difference between the two.

Odie sat on the shag rug in her dorm wrapped in a thin fleece blanket, Blackberry at her ear as she picked at the fuzz on her worn sweatpants. Massachusetts seemed colder now than it had ever been, even though the summer heat was only just waning into a milder autumn. The phone rang, a good sign, but no one answered.

She tried again two more times. On the third, a voice:

"...Hey, Sis. That you?"

"Hey, Momma. How's it going?"

Odie's voice trembled against her will, and she swallowed repeatedly to repress it. Her throat tightened and a stinging shot up her nostrils to her eyes, the sour threat of tears burning through her sinuses.

"Oh, it's goin'," Momma said.

Odie heard a thudding clicking she recognized: Momma's hand pulling at the handle of a gas pump, wanting to get the price right to the very cent to equal the change she had in her pocket.

"I'm with Travis right now. He's hidin' out from the law. I been driving his car. You remember Travis?"

"Uh-huh." Unfortunately. One of Momma's old boyfriends with a deeply pitted and pockmarked face, a beer belly that sat on his hips like a twin pregnancy. And the smell.

"Yeah, he ain't got his license or nothin'."

"That's not good." Odie looked down at her thumb, whittling away at the dead skin with her middle fingernail. She pulled at it too deep until the vulnerable living meat began to bleed.

"No, it ain't. I'm helping him out."

"By getting him out of town?"

"Yeah. Going down to Louisiana for a bit."

"How you gettin' back? You know I'm coming home for Thanksgiving, right?"

There was a pause on the other end of the line. Odie could hear the male voice in the background, gruff and irritable, and Momma pulled the phone away from her ear to give back as good as he gave. Then she was back.

"No, Sis, I didn't know that."

"So it means I won't see you when I come down, right?"

"Well, I don't know, Sis. Depends on if I got the money to get back right then, you know?"

"I haven't seen you in two years. You didn't even make it to my high school graduation."

Odie realized she'd forgotten why she'd called in the first place. She could still feel the rapist inside her, his hands groping her wrists and pinning them at her sides as her consciousness waned. She was thrust back there in the remembering, breath hitching.

"I know, Sis. I wish I'd known. You should have told me sooner."

"Uh-huh." She put her bleeding thumb in her mouth and sucked, taste of metal snaking down the back of her throat. She could hear Travis in the background again like a fussy patient, Momma's muffled placating.

"Can I call you back later, Sis? I gotta go. He's trying to drive and he ain't got no license."

"He's already running from the law, what difference does it make?"

Momma laughed.

"I love you, Sis. I gotta go!"

"I love you."

Odie said it back. Was it true? She didn't know. It felt true sometimes. She could hardly feel a thing for the hollowness inside her, resentment pouring into the cracks of her like swamp crud.

5

SHE SWALLOWED the gag tightening her throat and made a left turn into an empty gas station lot, parking the car at a haphazard angle over cracked and faded paint lines.

The inside of the gas station was cramped, shelves of Doritos and candy bars gathering dust in aisles that were almost too thin to pass through. Behind the counter, the teller sat perched high on a stool, his skin dark and leathery from too much sun and smelling of chewing tobacco. His grey eyes were yellowed and sticky and did not look away from the glitching, spider-webbed screen of his flip phone as he spoke.

"Bathroom's for customers only," he said before Odie could speak. "Minimum of ten on credit."

"So if I don't have cash, I have to pay ten dollars to use the bathroom?"

"Looks about that way."

His voice was gruff, low and slow, heavy with his accent, all hard R's and long vowels.

"More'n half the people that stops here need the bathroom. No regard for me'n mine nor the cost of water."

"Well, I'll pay after. It's an emergency."

"Always an emergency," he said, spinning on his stool to retrieve a key ring, weighed down by a large cowbell that rang brassily as he handed it over. "Minimum of ten, remember that, Princess."

She took the key and scanned the small store. The only other door was eggshell white, stained yellow by age and nicotine, paint cracked in rivulets up and down the length of the wood. She slipped inside and turned on the light. It flickered and lit up the closet space, everything cast in an orange glow. There was a short toilet and a roll of paper towels soaking on the damp floor, a spigot over a five-gallon bucket masquerading as a sink, and a piss smell that made her stomach flip and cramp again.

"Ten dollars my ass," Odie muttered.

Then she was gasping, undoing the drawstring of her sweatpants and sitting down on the toilet. The seat felt clammy as a frog's belly on her skin, and she gagged again as she peed, looking down at the red-soaked pad cradled in her underwear.

The stream became a thick drip. She parted her legs, watching the blood ooze and plop into the water.

At the clinic, they'd told her to take off work. Not to drive long distances. Plan to stay home for a few days while the pills worked. Process her feelings around the abortion, if she had any, and take it easy.

But it was Thanksgiving break, and there was no

time for that. And so there she was in a gas station 30 miles from Arkansas, having an abortion in a toilet with permanent skid marks in the bowl.

She leaned forward, sweat matting dark hair across her forehead as she placed her hand on the wall and pushed. Was she supposed to push? She didn't know.

The pressure dipped low in her gut, burning like dread, the kind that made her feel like she was going to shit herself, her eyes squeezing shut. A wet, metallic smell. A gummy feeling between her legs. And then the pressure was eased. She could breathe again, letting out a long hiss through her teeth.

She looked between her thighs, a bloody clump the shape of a raw egg settling at the bottom of the toilet bowl. Was that all it was? She wiped and wiped and replaced her pad, standing and bending her knees to get a better look.

The thing looked black under the orange light. Odie used the pin light on her keyring to light it up, turn it a darker red. She half-imagined she would see something like a cherub-lipped mouth, tiny fingers curled in a fist, or a tuft of feather-like hair in the mess of blood cradled in the bowl, but there was nothing resembling a human there. Just a small mess like a murder scene.

Odie couldn't explain the compulsion to touch it, to investigate it, but the intrusive thought whittled inside until her hand was in the water, scooping out the bloody clot. It reminded her of the elusive way the shard of an eggshell slipped through the jelly of an egg in a hot pan. It felt like snot, or the way a jellyfish might feel, and it quickly turned her skin a bright, watery red.

Odie spotted the trash can on its side, an empty water bottle half-crushed and spilled out onto the floor among wads of shit-stained paper.

She picked up the bottle, turned on the sputtering and coughing spigot, and filled it a quarter of the way with yellowed water. She funneled the jellied clot of would-be baby inside with her fingers in a fist, watching it drift down to the bottom. The sediment from the old pipes danced and fell around it like snow.

6

PLACES HAD SOULS, and this one was dying. The Arkansas plains were dry from drought, sidewalks cracked from too much heat and too much shifting of the earth beneath, plants stretching up from the confines of the asphalt like zombie fingers from a grave. They were starved of sunlight, of air that didn't feel heavy with humidity, of cool and crisp breezes, of a proper rain.

She passed the old gas station that used to be called Dandy Don's. They served the best homemade biscuits and gravy out of a crockpot. When she was small, Daddy would send her walking down a stretch of road for four Styrofoam containers filled to the brim with biscuits swimming in salty gravy. Now the gas station was a Quik Mart and the counter where they served the biscuits and gravy had been replaced with toaster ovens lined with dripping frozen pizzas, too hot and chemical yellow.

There was the Old Rialto theatre, a historic landmark in the downtown area with an Art Deco-style neon marquee. It had been there for nearly 100 years. Her family called it the poor folk theater because it was the only one they could afford.

Her home wasn't in the town proper like it had been when she was younger, near the old music store and the old toy shop and the little hole-in-the-wall Mom and Pop breakfast joint that opened at 5:00 a.m. and closed at 10:00 a.m.

Odie's family lived on the outskirts of town, down a winding dirt road shaded dark by trees. The house smelled of mildew and the foundation put the whole thing at a tilt. The ceilings were low. Everything felt narrow and shut-in like a shed, and millipedes populated the shower drains. Cats with mange and kittens dying of respiratory illnesses lived in hordes under the baby blue trailer next door, and the whole place smelled of soil and rot. She had been ashamed to live there.

Her throat tightened as she took the highway out to the other side of town. More cramps. Dread, or perhaps aftershocks of the abortion, like the ghost of an earthquake come to remind her a rift had formed, two halves colliding and tearing a new scar inside her.

She did not like to remember this house. She did not like to return there. She did not like the threat of roaches touching her skin, or the crampedness of the kitchen, or the way they all had to eat sitting on the living room floor, shoulder-to-shoulder, bumping into each other like cattails in a windstorm.

She wanted desperately to turn the car around.

Then she was rocking along a gravel road and

turning down a dirt one. She bumped along the deep gashes left by the wear of tires in the sopping earth, spinning in the ground water that collected there, her car lurching forward again with a great heave. She passed tin trailers decorated with the saddles of long-dead horses, bullet-hole riddled cans scattered in the dead grass. Finally, at the end of the road, she came to the small house she had left behind, the small house in which her family lived with the millipedes and roaches. A bull's skull hung from the mailbox by a twisted nail, horns at a tilt.

7

HER DADDY WAS WAITING at the screen door.

Odie switched off the hatchback's ignition, the engine hissing with an exhausted sigh. The door opened with a creak as she pulled herself out, taking a few unsteady steps toward Daddy as his green, bloodshot eyes swam in a mist of tears. There was a tug on her heart, blood calling to blood.

Daddy had to duck to descend the waterlogged steps of the cluttered front porch. His arms were open and her arms were open, and then they collided. She was against his belly, face pressed to his chest, inhaling the sweet menthol scent of his chewing tobacco and the hoppy smell of cheap beer, the biting undercurrent of vodka. For just a moment, she forgot her reluctance to come home, because home was not a place as much as it was a feeling, and the feeling was love, love, love.

"Papa Bear." Odie's nose tingled with the threat of tears. She pulled away to look up at him, blinking them away. His were streaming down his face. "Hell's bells, don't you get me crying now. You have me for a whole week, and we're gonna make the most of it."

He was a rough thing. He was drunk, but he'd tried to cover the smell with Old Spice. He didn't know how red his eyes were. He didn't know how he couldn't pretend.

"Oh, I missed you so!" He gripped Odie again, tighter, his hot mouth on her shoulder as he began to shake with sobs. It had only been three months, yet her absence upset him to his core. "I'm so happy you're here."

"Did you remember my one request? Did you make my fried cabbage?"

"Well, hell yeah. Of course I did."

He wiped his nose with the back of his hand and a long sniff.

Over Daddy's shoulder, Bubba was standing on the top step of the porch, the wood sinking beneath the weight of his heavy work boots. He was shirtless, his skin browned. She knew he'd taken a job in the rice fields. He looked like a man.

He took the three steps down at once with his long legs, taking his turn for a hug. His was firm, his face burying against Odie's shoulder the same way Daddy's did, but Bubba didn't cry.

"I sure did miss ya."

His breath was bitter with nicotine smell.

"Missed you too, Bub."

She rubbed the knobby road of his spine, the angel's wings of his shoulder blades beneath his tanned skin.

Bubba Tucker was a Southern boy through and

through, rough around the edges and only rougher as he grew, heart hardening to the world as it became more and more punishing to the softness of boys. At 17, he had already had his first stint in rehab for meth, had been arrested for burglary and assault, was expecting his first child with someone Odie had never met. Yet in her arms, despite his towering height over her, he was the same baby boy she had first held at her mother's bedside, marveling at the feat of him, at the fact that he had grown from nothing and had magically appeared in the world to make her a big sister.

"Where's Denise?"

"Hey, Baby Girl." Odie's stepmother had been lingering at the screen door, watching her homecoming. Her bleached hair was a tangled tumbleweed sitting directly atop her head. Her skin was pallid, eyes darkly lined with smudged coal. Her bare arm had a ring of bruises around it, the thickness of Daddy's fingers. "How you doin', Sweetheart? Been a long time, it feels like!"

She too embraced Odie, but was met with the detached puppetry of a hug. It wasn't that Denise had ever harmed Odie or committed some unforgivable transgression, nor had she ever been anything other than victim to her father's drunken abuses, to Odie's knowledge anyway.

But Denise was her father's fifth wife, and one of many women who had come and gone. It was best to keep a distant heart. Though they had been married for two years, it made little difference to Odie. She knew what would last and what would not, and when it came to Daddy, nothing *ever* lasted.

"Hey, Denise. Good to see you." Odie gave a tight smile, taking great care to make it reach her eyes. "This everyone?"

"Who else would there be?" Daddy gave an impish grin, his missing front tooth showing.

Denise elbowed him before taking his large hand in hers and dragging him up the porch.

"Come on in, Sweetheart. We got cabbage and a pot of beans on the stove."

"After we eat, I'll show you my squirrel tails," Bubba called over his shoulder, one foot already in the door.

"I don't think I want anything to do with squirrel tails."

"I got ten of 'em on a string."

"Gross."

Bubba disappeared into the dark house.

Night was falling. She could feel the mosquitoes brushing against her skin like eyelashes, the little sting of their mouths drawing blood. She swatted at the back of her neck, her eyes on the darkened edge that led to the far side of the house, and beyond that the tall grass that buttressed the perimeter of the property.

Her hearing broke past the songs the crickets sang, her vision straining through a web of fireflies drifting like dust in a beam of sunlight. But she heard nothing but the sounds of the Arkansas night, saw nothing but the desolate landscape turn eerily peaceful and alien with its nocturnal insects.

She ducked her head back in her car, taking the

water bottle and stuffing it inside her messenger bag, careful to secure it with the zipper. She couldn't leave it out here, she didn't know why. Fall nights in Arkansas were humid as ever, but the temperature could drop low. Odie heard some folks could die of hypothermia in the desert, and she imagined Arkansas was much the same.

She circled the car to pull her bag out of the hatchback, but her throat was quickly strangled by a cinch, pulling her back hard. She felt the sharp stab of a gun's barrel in her ribs, a voice hushed and quick in her ear.

"Don't you fuckin' move."

8

ODIE TURNED SHARPLY, the grip of the arm around her throat falling. She was in her assailant's arms, a hop drawing her legs up around the attacker's waist as they both fell. Her hand was still holding the shape of a gun with her thumb, pointer, and middle fingers, pressing it to the dip of Odie's clavicle.

"I knew it," Odie said, wrestling Dale's wrists to the ground while she bucked and kicked beneath her.

Eventually, Dale was able to get the upper hand, her long legs flexible enough to twist over Odie's head and push her flat on her back. Dale's hands scrambled for Odie's arms and sat on them with her knees, both girls panting and laughing even as Odie struggled.

"I knew you were here. My spider senses were tingling."

"Isn't it supposed to be *spidey* senses? What else was tingling?"

Dale drew her tongue over Odie's cheek like a lapping dog. Odie twisted her face away and Dale finally let up, dropping off to the side to lay beside her in the damp grass. Laying there on their backs, she could almost feel the earth worms in the damp soil. She could also feel several pieces of gravel digging into her vertebrae.

"You're disgustin'." Odie smacked Dale's chest.

"Miss me, Big Shot?"

"Yeah. About as much as I missed Denise."

"That's not very nice. Denise never done nothing to you."

They lay there giggling, looking at each other in the dark. Behind the car, no one could see them.

"What's it like up there in Mass-a-two-shits these days?"

"Fine."

"Fine? Don't sound that good. Don't sound good enough to leave all this behind."

Dale waved her hand around her head, her eyes rolling up to view the dirt road upside down.

"Yeah, there was so much keeping me here. I miss the mosquitoes."

Dale was quiet for a moment at that, the darkness hiding her pinched expression. Then: "They're called 'skeeters.' Y'all skeet skeet, motherfuckers!"

"You're such a dumbass."

Dale sat up, smoothing her hair back. It was long and dark, dyed black with a cheap box from Dollar General. It was freshly done, Odie could tell, but she'd missed a spot of white-blonde hair at the roots. There was a chemical taste to the air near Dale's face, the familiar sickly sweet aroma of the conditioner that came with the dye kit.

"Your hair looks nice," Odie said. "Smells like something I'd mop the floor with, but it looks nice."

"Yours looks like shit. I need to do your roots while you're down."

"I'm thinking of shaving it all off. I'm tired of it."

Odie ruffled her own hair. It was short already, sticking up at odd ends, with a perpetual cow lick.

"Your daddy won't like that. He already thinks your hair makes you look queer."

"Well, he's not wrong."

9

2003

ODIE DIDN'T KNOW black hair soaked up heat like lizard skin, so the first time she dyed her hair the color of tar the sweat ran down her temples dark as ink. She sat on top of the brick sign outside middle school with a bejeweled CD player in her lap, the soft sponge of her headphones soaking in the running dye. She wiped and wiped at the sweat with the back of her hand, the sun relentless, right on the cusp of summer.

"What are you listening to?"

The question came from her left, muffled by the tinny music blaring from the dollar store headphones. She recognized Dahlia Stevens from around school, but they'd never spoken. Her white-blonde hair and eyebrows glittered in the sunlight like snowflakes, a spattering of freckles across her nose and her large blue eyes giving her a fawn-like appearance.

There were rumors that Dahlia was a dyke. She had a boyish slouch.

Odie lifted one speaker from her ear, cocking a brow that itched with runny dye.

"Huh?"

"I asked what you're listening to," she repeated, motioning toward the CD player, letting her hand drop back down to her side.

"Oh. That new band, Evanescence. Their album's out. Have you heard of them?"

"Duh, of course I'm heard of them," Dahlia said. "How'd you get that? My momma signed that petition to get it taken out of stores here. She said it's devil music."

Odie scoffed softly, pulling her headphones down around her neck, the music still rattling against her skin, Amy Lee's crescendo, the scratch of the electric guitar, the thump of the drums like a hammer.

"I downloaded it on LimeWire. My neighbor just got Internet and he burned a CD for me. I can make you one, if you want. Just hide it from your momma."

Dahlia pulled herself up next to Odie on the brick sign, kicking her feet, which were clothed in black Converse high tops. She had taken a Sharpie and drawn a black and white checkerboard on the rubber toes of the shoes. The shoestrings were black and neon green, crisscrossed across the top of her foot in the shape of a pentagram.

Odie held her foot out to show off her own, identical except for the shoelaces, which were pink.

"We almost match."

Dahlia held her foot out next to Odie's.

"Did you know Amy Lee is from Little Rock?"

"Duh."

"You're Odette, right?"

"Everyone calls me Odie. Odette don't feel right. Feels like something you'd call an old lady."

"I get it. I want everyone at school to call me Dale, but I don't want my folks to find out. They'd say it's a boy's name, or something stupid like that. They're real hung up on 'boy' stuff and 'girl' stuff."

Odie shrugged, kicking her heels against the brick wall, scuffing the backs of her shoes.

"I'll call you Dale if you want."

"Just not around my momma, okay? She won't like it."

"I never met your momma."

Dale gave Odie a big grin, the first of its kind, and one she'd seen many times since.

"You will. You're coming over, right?"

10

2005

THE FIRST TIME Odie cut her hair short, Dale had done it for her at a sleepover. When Odie came home the next afternoon, she brought Dale with her, because Daddy was always nicer when someone else was around.

Daddy was sitting in his recliner when they came in, the screen door slamming behind them. It was tornado season, and the wind had come and gone all day, at one point making the tin roof flutter like and eyelid.

"...The hell you do to your head?"

"Gave Odie a haircut," Dale said, running her hand back and forth over the shorn locks atop Odie's scalp. "You like it?"

They sat on the sofa, old fabric drenched in nicotine and menthol smell. Daddy looked at them as if he were trying to think of something funny to say, the words dancing at the edge of his tipsy brain.

"Y'all look gay," he said at last, as if he'd given up searching for something more clever the longer the silence hung between them. "Y'all gay together or somethin'?"

"Hey, I'm a dyke, get it right."

Dale's voice took on a tone of mock defensiveness, her blue eyes good-natured. Strong. Fearless.

"Hell, I know what you are, but I never been so sure about Odie. I been suspicious. You ain't got the face for short hair, Odette. It's ugly on you. Tell me the truth, you a dyke, too?"

"I think I'm bisexual, Daddy."

His light eyes grew dark, the perpetual red of the whites deepening almost to crimson with the shadowy tuck of his chin. He was no longer playfully probing, but hardened in the certainty of what he had always expected and feared.

"You think you're what?"

Silence again, this time broken by Denise surfacing from the back bedroom in a plume of skunk smoke.

"Odette says she's a lesbian now," Daddy said.

"Oh, Baby Girl, that's against God."

Denise's reply was quick, but Odie sensed in it a kind of dismissal, that Denise didn't really care who she was attracted to one way or the other. It was a response to appease Daddy, to ease the tension in the room that grew with his disgust.

Daddy put the stool down on his recliner, his big body making like it was going to stand, the liquid in his beer can sloshing with the suddenness of his movement. Daddy floundered to his feet, unsteady on his swollen ankles.

"Git, you two. Odette, if you wanna look like a man and be with women, that's your choice, but I better not see you around here with no girl, or else."

"Or else what? You'll get your shotgun?"

"I might!" His shout was quick as a snake bite, and like a snake he reared back, as if to take the bite back after the poison had already set. "I don't know!"

Odie had expected resistance. She had even expected him to send her away. A small part of her had hoped he'd shrug the revelation off, but she hadn't counted on it. She thought surely she'd prepared herself for every scenario, when the day came that she finally told him.

Dale moved to hold Odie's hand, but Odie shook her off.

"Let's just go, Odie, if he's gonna be like that."

Dale took Odie's hand again, grasping it tightly, not allowing her to pull away. Dale tugged her toward the door.

"You ought to be ashamed," Dale said to Daddy.

"Y'all ought to be ashamed!" Daddy waved his hand at Dale wildly, dismissing them both. "Git, I said!"

The screen door slammed behind them as they made their way out back, into the tall, tall weeds behind the house, where the grasshoppers were croaking good morning in the dew.

Odie let Dale's hand go, walking at a clip ahead of her, the dawn air burning her lungs. For the first time she let herself feel the disappointment and rage spitting inside like a firework, tearing the soft tissue of her into raw strips.

"He don't mean nothing," Dale said, stopping at the edge of the backyard, where the brambles got too thick to walk. "None of this means nothing. He's gonna come around, Odette. That man loves you."

Odie looked back over her shoulder, could see Daddy's shadow behind the thatched steel gray of the back screen door. When he noticed her looking, he slammed the door closed so hard the whole house rattled.

"He loves the parts of me he wants to love. He loves the parts of me that can live with the kind of father he is, the parts that forgive his drunk ass time and time again!"

"We're just kids, Odie. He's the daddy, he should be better than that. None of it's your fault, and he's gonna see that someday. He's gonna lose you, and he'll know it's him who done that, not you."

Odie looked up at Dale, tears clinging to her eyelashes like dew to a blade of grass. Then her gaze lifted to the trees growing up in the brambles, thickening into a forest that stretched way back yonder, farther back than they could ever go.

"There's snakes in them trees, Dale. Look."

Dale followed Odie's gaze to low-hanging branches, cracking from the thrashing of two snakes. Their muscles twisted around the branches and each other, rippling under their rough scales. One of the snakes was brown and striped, its head thick and snout snubbed. The other was slick and black, speckled yellow.

There was little time to react before the thin branch the snakes were twisted around collapsed and came down atop Odie's head. She felt the creatures thrashing against her freshly cut hair, her cheeks, her shoulders. Then they dropped heavy at her feet.

Dale and Odie both let out a scream, grasping at each other as they ran back toward the house, hollering.

Daddy came out the screen door, stomping down the sagging back steps, his voice already breathless.

"What is it?"

"Daddy, there was snakes in the trees back there! They're fighting, and they fell out the tree onto my head!"

"Grab the hoe," he said, setting his beer down on top of the septic tank, balancing it atop the peak of the cylinder so it wouldn't spill. Odie handed him the hoe, then followed him back to the brambles. The snakes were still there, bodies hopelessly tangled and stretched mouths locked to each other's necks.

Daddy hit the brown snake's tail with the hoe, the tangled bodies jumping with the force as it half-severed. Blood fed the soil. He pushed their bodies over, using the edge of the gardening tool to try to pry them apart.

"Stay back, Odette. That brown one there's a copperhead. The other one's a kingsnake. That's the one that ain't poisonous."

Both Dale and Odie recoiled, clinging to each other and watching Daddy work the tool between the snake bodies, using a sharp edge to stab and cut at the copperhead while the black and yellow kingsnake untangled itself from the pieces. Finally, bloodied and bitten, the kingsnake retreated into the brambles, its slither a little sideways, disoriented. The pieces of the copperhead still thrashed and twitched.

"Don't worry, girls. It's dead. Them's just death throes."

"What about the kingsnake? Won't it die from the venom? It's all bit to hell," Dale said, the black and yellow tail disappearing completely into the thickets, leaving a dark trail of blood.

"Kingsnakes are immune to venom. Kingsnakes eat other snakes up, that's why I didn't kill him."

Daddy swung the hoe a final time, chopping off the copperhead's head. The disembodied piece flopped like a fish, mouth gaping, the yellow eye wide and the slit drawn into a sliver.

Odie never mentioned her sexuality again, and Daddy never did talk about it neither.

11

ODIE KNEW her father had been drinking by the redness in his eyes. He always started out boisterous. He would put his thick arm over her shoulders, the weight causing her to sink into the carpet.. He would sing or joke close to her ear, the menthol smell of the chewing tobacco on his breath washing over her face.

In eighth grade, she and her peers had learned that dip was seven times more likely to cause cancer in the mouth and throat than cigarettes. She learned about all the little micro tears from the glass in the tobacco that occurred inside the dip-filled lip, and she imagined these in her daddy's mouth, perpetual taste of blood, endless pain he couldn't feel.

When the boisterousness passed, Daddy, red-faced and gasping for air, would grow quiet and stare off, his eyes welling up, cheeks swelling as he rubbed at them furiously.

She could tell she had taken too long getting home, had missed the happy one-man celebration Daddy had in anticipation of seeing his eldest return from college. He was now tearful and clingy, hovering around her and staring as if she were so beautiful and so sad.

"Stop staring at me," Odie said.

"I can't help it. You're just so damn grown up. I'm so proud of you. Look how pretty you are. So smart. So talented. Ain't I the luckiest man in the world? Praise God, he gave you to me."

She had considered telling him about her rape, about the abortion, about all of it.

She wanted what she'd had when she was small, right after her parents had divorced and it was just her, Daddy, and Bubba in a ramshackle trailer sitting on a farm property. They'd shared a bedroom and a bed and fed the hogs five-gallon buckets of crabapples in exchange for shelter. At that time, Daddy was only 25 years old, and she felt she could tell him anything, laying in bed on a Saturday morning as he spun stories out of thin air.

She wanted that kind of comfort, that kind of familiarity, but when Daddy was like this, he felt like a stranger. Not a happy man. Not a man at all. A wounded child, his adulthood diluted by vodka and time and bitterness.

Odie took a beer from the fridge, eyeing Daddy to see if he'd tell her to put it back. When he just smiled sadly, she popped the Bud Light open with a cat's hiss from the can.

"I'm sorry I didn't give you a better life." His voice broke, his broad shoulders sinking in a soft sob.

"Why are you saying that?" Odie took a long drink,

letting the foul piss-water burn in her stomach. Her free hand moved to cover his calloused fingers. "Where is the coming from?"

"I could have, if it weren't for this."

He nudged his own beer across the countertop hard, the can tipping precariously close to the edge before snapping upright with the slosh of the liquid within.

"Shhh, Daddy. I just got here. This is a happy time."

Odie abandoned her beer and circled to the other side of the counter, putting her arms around Daddy and pulling him close. She had to stand on her tiptoes to do this, to bring his head to her shoulder, and he heaved another sob into her shirt, grasping her and letting his weight settle in a way that caused her to stumble sideways.

"Hey, hey. It's okay. Why don't you lay down, huh? It's been a long day for both of us."

She ran her fingers through his graying hair, which was soft and thinning.

"I don't want to lay down," he said, his inhale hitching, his eyes a spider web of capillaries over the jaundiced, sticky whites. "I want you to understand."

He clutched his hands in her T-shirt, and she had a sudden flashback to her childhood, all the times he'd done this in anger, pulling her up by her collar and gritting his teeth at her little nose. Muscle memory tensed her up like a rabbit, her heart jumping into her throat even though there was no threat now, just a weeping mess of a man who'd spent the day simmering in his grief.

"I do understand, Daddy," she said quietly, setting

her beer down and holding his wrists in loose, placating fists. "I know you love me. You always have and always will. You did the best you could with what you had, and I'm grateful."

His grip eased, and he nodded, wrapping his arms around Odie again and pulling her against his chest, cheek pressed over the dome of her head as he rocked side to side.

"I love you so much. I just love you so much."

"I know. I promise, I know."

He stood there for a moment longer before releasing her and taking a great, hot breath.

"Goddamn," he said, wiping his eyes again and forcing a soft, self-effacing laugh. "It's been a day."

"For me, too," she agreed, picking up her beer again as he lifted his.

Together they took a long drink. Odie tipped her head back, staring into the orange glow of the moth-covered kitchen light.

12

THIS IS why she didn't like to come home. She could not live in the present here. She could not see her feet in front of her or picture the next day or the next. Every moment pulled her deeper into the past, deeper into the land, and the more she struggled, the more she sank.

13

HER FIRST NIGHT HOME, Odie didn't sleep. Dale stayed over, even though Odie was exhausted from her drive, and she listened to the sound of her deep breathing, in and out, smooth as the sighing water at a pond's edge.

She considered telling Dale about what had happened, about the water bottle she'd hidden inside her dresser and the amoebic tissues floating within and how the thing came to be inside her in the first place. But it wasn't something she had told anyone, and she didn't know if she could.

14

IN THE QUIET is when she thought about it most, in the dark. Odie wasn't small, and yet the boy who had held her wrists could do it with a single hand. The alcohol in her system had helped, and the switch in her head that flipped when she realized what was being done to her. Everything had gone black and silent after he forced himself inside her, and the only thing she remembered after that, before waking, was the vague impression of his fingers wandering her body and his burning breath licking at her like a flame.

15

SHE CHECKED the time on her Blackberry: a quarter to four. There was a light spattering of rain on the tin roof, thumping overhead like a maraca. She lay there listening, letting it lull her, the smell of wet earth drifting in through the cracked window.

SCRAAAAPE.

Odie opened her eyes, lifting her head from the pillow to free her other ear. The sound was low and it was in her room, she was certain of it. Odie had seen many millipedes and roaches sheltering in the old ramshackle house, had even seen a few mice, but she didn't think that was a sound any of those little strangers would make.

SCRAPE. THUMP.

The sound of wood on wood, the sound of a stuck drawer struggling to open, the sound of someone releasing it in defeat.

Odie slipped out from under the covers and placed her feet on the bare, cracked linoleum. The dresser was less than two feet away in the cramped room. The middle drawer was cracked an inch and canted at an angle as if it had been pulled unevenly. She ran her fingers inside, finding the water bottle with her abortion in it where she'd left it. It had fallen on its side, the cap unscrewed, and the abortion had worked its way to the short neck of the bottle. The old softball jerseys she'd placed over it had fallen to the side, a few blooms from the leakage soaked into the fabric. She put the cap back on and pushed the bottle to the back of the drawer again, stuffing the shirts over it.

16

HAD someone been in her room?

When she'd gotten her wisdom teeth removed, Bubba had stolen her hydrocodone. He was only 15 at the time. Maybe he was looking for pills again, thinking she was asleep. It would have been risky with her and Dale there.

She scraped the drawer back into place, the wood groaning. Dale groaned.

"What're you doing?"

"Nothing. I think Bubba was in here," Odie whispered.

"Fapping?"

"Gross. Never say that again." She climbed back beneath the quilt and turned on her side, eyes on the vague ghost of Dale's pale face. "Maybe he was looking for something he left in here while I was away."

"Mm. I don't see why it couldn't wait until morning. What time is it?"

"Almost four."

"God. Go back to sleep, Odie."

"I haven't even been to sleep yet. It's too weird being back. It feels like stepping back in time, to a place I tried so hard to get away from. I'm happy to see you, Dale. I love you, I love my family... I just hate it here. Dale...?"

Dale snorted softly, her lips slightly open as air hissed through her parted teeth. Odie closed her eyes and drifted in and out of memories, but she didn't fall asleep and the scraping did not return.

17

"BUBBA, were you in my room last night?"

Odie was leaning in the narrow doorway of his bedroom. He was sitting on the edge of his bed, sharpening the edge of a thin, jagged rock against a larger, smooth stone. He'd been trying to make his own arrowheads, chipping away at the work in his usual quiet way.

"Don't reckon I was, unless I've taken to sleepwalking. Why?"

"I dunno. I heard something, I thought it might'a been you."

"What'd it sound like?"

"Like a drawer opening. The middle drawer of my dresser was open a little."

"Oh, yeah, I know what that was."

He went back to scraping stone on stone, the sound clean, like the tearing of a thin sheet of paper.

"What?"

"There's a big fat possum that lives in here by the

name of Randy. It was him." He looked back up at her, giving a crooked, yellowed grin. "He's been going around opening drawers, sniffing all our underwear."

She felt a pang in her heart at how much she'd missed him.

18

Baby

DARK AND QUIET. Baby didn't know why it was so dark and quiet and wet. It had taken great effort to unscrew the cap on the water bottle a second time. Baby was exhausted, dancing in the stale fluid. A sticky tendril lashed out of the bottle's mouth, reaching, reaching, like one of those sticky hands from a coin-operated toy machine. Baby's tendril tightened into a claw, feeling and tapping its way around the inside of the drawer. It sounded like a jagged fingernail scratching the inside of a coffin, scritch scritch scritch.

The dresser groaned when Baby wrapped itself into a ball and hit the inner wall of the drawer, causing it to jump with a thud. Baby was like a bullet, fast and sharp. Baby collided over and over until the smallest sliver of air hit its amoebic body.

The opening wasn't as big as the one Baby had made two nights ago, but no matter. Baby would make it work. Baby squeezed its tendril out of the crack, wriggling like a worm breaking from the earth during a lightning storm. Reaching, reaching, touching the outside of the dresser with a wet slap.

Baby pushed and pushed, sucking in its body with a soft slurp, elongating, stretching thin until Baby could slip through the crack, tumbling out onto the floor. Baby didn't need breath, but lay there undulating as if panting, laying there for some time before stretching its 'hand' forward and inching along the linoleum.

The room was so small, but to Baby it seemed enormous. Bigger than womb and toilet bowl and dresser drawer, bigger than water bottle. Baby left a little blood trail in its wake, thin and pink, circling around the bed and 'sniffing' like a dog. Exploring. Baby had a sense of where it wanted to go.

The old wooden frame of Odie's twin bed stood like a great cliff's edge, one that Baby would have to scale. Baby didn't have a sense of time, only determination. The hours eked by, Baby silent and slithering. Finally on the bed, Baby's moistness sank into the fabric, leaving pink and red splotches. Baby wrapped itself into a ball and tumbled over the sheet, rolling like a tumble weed between Odie's feet. Baby made its way between Odie's thighs until they became too thick, too close together to navigate, then stretched out long again to wriggle up to her groin.

Baby 'sniffed' with its tendril, curious, exploring the dark warmth of Odie's pubic hair. It parted the hair like an explorer, forging a path between thick brush. Odie inhaled softly in her sleep, shifting and jostling Baby, but Baby was already between Odie's lips.

Odie's eyes fluttered open when Baby slithered inside her vagina, squeezing her thighs together, reaching between her legs to scratch the strange itch just as Baby's last ligament disappeared inside her. Odie sat up suddenly, feeling between her legs with prodding fingers as Baby moved further into her vaginal cavity, breaking through to her cervix with a whisper of pain.

She held her belly and groaned, cramping and turning to press the top of her head into the pillow, doubled over. She could feel something low in her abdomen, dancing and pinging off the fragile walls inside her. Trickles of blood seeped into her panties.

When the pain eased, a complacent exhaustion overtook her limbs, heavy and full as a bladder. She sank back onto the bed, her lips parted in panting sighs, her eyes rolling as her nerve endings sang with the strange electricity of life. Her arms became limp at her sides, her doubled-over body falling over into the fetal position, her fingers twitching. Then it all went black.

19

THE NEXT MORNING, Odie felt sore and strange. Her white cotton underwear was soaked with blood, through the sheets and into the old mattress. When she moved she felt stiff, and when she stretched her joints popped in their cartilage fixings.

Her mouth felt dry. She could hear pots and pans, smell the strong scent of frying bacon. Her stomach growled, beast-like, and she pulled herself from the tangle of the blankets and shuffled her bare feet through the small house.

It was standing room only in the kitchen, too small for a table and chairs. The family had to camp in the living room in front of the TV during meals.

"Mornin'." Daddy was at the stove, the pink raw-side up of the bacon bubbling on top of the grease.

"Where's Denise?"

Odie leaned against the counter next to her dad, pulling her long nightshirt down over her knees.

"Laying down."

Laying down never meant sleeping. Sleeping meant sleeping. Laying down meant she was in a pill coma. Odie probably wouldn't see her again until after it got dark, and maybe not even then. Odie's stomach let out a growl.

"Hungry, Odette?"

"More than usual."

"You've lost a little weight since we last saw you."

Odie hummed at that, dismissive. She didn't want to talk about her weight. Not now, not ever.

Daddy flipped the bacon over, the fried side dark and stiff, little pieces of cracked smoke clinging to it. Odie felt her stomach clench, her hand going low on her abdomen. She couldn't pinpoint what the feeling was, if it was hunger or a cramp or something else. What she did know was that she was starving, starving to the point it felt maddening, her jaws aching with sour and her lips wet with saliva.

"I don't care if it's done, put it on a plate," she said, drool clinging to her lip. She'd never been so hungry in all her life.

20

ODIE WAS restless like carpet moth larvae spinning on silk strings. Her body was itchy and strange, as if a layer of her skin had separated and become a shadow, all her moving parts really moving, water boiling over the lip of a pot, a sudden wind bowling over wild onions.

She stood in the bathroom, staring at two millipedes circling the shower drain like carousel horses. She didn't know how long she'd been standing there watching them until she was jerked out of her stupor by a rap at the door.

"I need in there, Sis," Bubba complained. "Gotta take a shit. I'm turtle-heading real bad out here."

Odie quickly flushed the toilet and turned on the sink, making like she was washing her hands. When she opened the door, Bubba was flushed.

"You're sick."

"How else was you supposed to know it's an emergency?"

Bubba passed her with a crooked-toothed grin.

Daddy was standing in front of the TV, shifting his weight on his feet.

"Hey, Sweetheart," he said, motioning at the screen. "See that? Flat screen TV, mounted on the wall and everything. Ain't it cool?"

"Talk about an upgrade."

"Want to go for a ride?"

"Out where?"

Odie hated being in the car with her dad, which was a shame, because he loved being in the car with Odie. Daddy's favorite hobby was riding down gravel roads and seeing what dust he could kick up. Other families had world travel, Florida vacations, or, at the very least, a yearly trip up to Branson, Missouri to visit Silver Dollar City. Odie's family had adventures down dirt roads across the endless plains and swamps of Arkansas, looking for new swimming holes, fishing spots, or wild blackberries to plunder.

"I don't want to be gone all day. I wanted to hang out with Dale later."

"Dale can come, too. You know I ain't seen you in a while."

He said it casually, but there was an edge in his voice only she could detect, the thing inside him that wanted her to feel guilty for doing anything without him. When he was half-sober, he could layer that cutting edge with subtlety, but when he was blackout drunk, it cut surgically.

You don't love me. You never did. You should go live with your mother.

An hour later, they were pulling out of the driveway.

21

WHEN THEY REACHED THE HIGHWAY, Daddy turned the opposite way from town. Bubba sat in the passenger's seat and Dale and Odie sat together in the back, taking turns looking out the windows at the farmland rolling by and texting each other in sly silence.

"Where are we going?" Dale asked.

"It's no fun if you know. Hell, I don't even know."

Daddy steadied the steering wheel with his knee, taking a long swig from a fifth of vodka and chasing it with a pull from a can of Coke. Bubba glanced at Odie and Odie glanced at Dale.

"Keep your hands on the wheel. That shit makes me nervous."

Dale was able to pal around with Daddy, especially when he was drunk, but there was a seriousness to her tone and a twist in all their stomachs.

It was a gray day, the clouds heavy with moisture and stretched out over the land. Odie could remember days like this from her childhood, which felt so long ago but wasn't, looking out over empty fields and imagining tornadoes spinning like tops across the plains. She'd actually seen her fair share of them; one almost took the roof off the tin trailer she, Daddy, and Bubba had lived in many years ago, right after her parents's divorce. She recalled the clattering like infant hands beating the keys of an unstrung piano, the discordant thrum of fear pattering like rain in her chest. Even powdery dust tornadoes sweeping across dry peanut fields reminded her of that night.

They stopped at a lone gas station off the highway where Daddy knew the chicken gizzards were good. They ordered two cardboard sleeves of gizzards and a sleeve of fried livers for Odie, the little morsels soaked in vegetable oil, the crispy crackling fry skins flaking off on their fingers as they passed them around and ate on the road. Gizzards were gray, tough, and chewy, salty and explosive in flavor. The livers were silky soft like mousse under the fried batter, a strong taste that permeated the sinus cavities. Fried chicken organs were a staple of everyday life and also a thing of immense nostalgia for Odie, reminding her of countless similar trips with Daddy through the countryside. When he cooked chicken at home, he would peel out the heart and give it to Odie to eat.

"I don't know how y'all can eat that."

Dale wrinkled her nose as Odie licked oil from her fingers. Daddy reached back over his seat, a thick gizzard pinched in front of Dale's face.

"Try it, it's good for you!"

Dale recoiled, wrinkling her nose up, lips pursed as she shook her head emphatically.

"No, and keep both hands on the wheel, damn it!"

She pushed his hand away lightly, and Daddy laughed, popping the organ into his mouth like candy.

22

AFTER A WHILE, when the clouds finally decided to part and let a little sunlight through, Daddy turned the car down a gravel road at random. The ditches lining it were grown up with weeds nearly eight feet tall, arching over the car in a claustrophobic hug. The area seemed seldom traveled and thick with trees, the bark coated in lavender-colored paint to warn trespassers away.

"No trespassing, Daddy," Odie said.

"It's a free country, ain't it? It don't look like anyone lives out here."

"Or they do, and they don't like company."

"You worry too much, Sis." Bubba turned around in his seat, offering the last gizzard, which lay at the bottom of the small cardboard carton, cold and shriveled. She shook her head, and he shrugged. "I won't let nothing bad happen to ya."

"If you're between me and a gun, the gun's gonna win," she muttered, looking out the window and squinting through the plant life for any sign they weren't alone.

The farther they ventured down the road, the thinner the weeds became, the trees spreading out like exhaling lungs, all the little pine-needle paths winding through their sturdy trunks widening so the sun could kiss the earth.

"Hey, look at that," Dale said, sitting up between the front seats and pointing ahead at a worn tire path off the side of the road. A field stretched out below a bright sky. "Is that corn?"

"Sure is. No one's harvested it, neither." Daddy slowed the car down, pulling it off to the side of the ditch and putting it in park with the engine still purring. "It'd be nice to have some of that fresh corn for Thanksgiving, don't you think, Bub?"

"Don't it belong to somebody?"

"We'll just dip in and out. We don't need much, and hell, they got plenty!" Daddy opened his car door before Odie could protest, and Bubba followed. Dale opened her door, but Odie grasped her wrist, shaking her head.

"What are you doing? We're gonna get shot if we go out there."

"Relax, Odie. I didn't see a house nowhere. I don't think anyone's around. We'll be quick."

She pulled her wrist free, this time taking Odie's hand and tugging her out the door.

"Are we just gonna leave the car running?" she shouted at Daddy, but he was long gone, disappeared through the rows of corn stalks. She huffed and let Dale drag her into the maze, her feet scuffing through the tilled dirt.

She could hear the cracking of the plants as Daddy and Bubba moved through the field somewhere off in the distance, could hear the sharp snap when one of them managed to pop an ear from the stalk. Dale pulled Odie close and kissed her cheek before shoving her back and taking off through the rustling leaves.

"Hey!" Odie shouted, annoyed, at least at first.

When the surprise wore off, she could hear Dale cackling.

"Marco!"

"Dale, come on. We shouldn't split up out here!"

The rows were becoming disorienting, as grating as fluorescent lights in a Walmart. Odie felt her head ache and her stomach churn, that childhood fear welling up that she would be lost out here forever, never to be found.

"I didn't hear you!" Dale shouted back, somewhere diagonal from the last place Odie had heard her voice.

"Fucking hell." Odie rolled her eyes, running in the direction of Dale's voice. "Polo! Fuck!"

"Marco!"

Closer, but Dale had zig-zagged, had ended up somewhere straight ahead from Odie. She could see Dale's legs disappear into another row, and Odie gave chase, her heart pounding and a little thrill zipping down her legs. She was going full speed now, her hands held like horse blinders beside her face to protect her eyes from drooping corn leaves and exploding silks, shouldering stalks out of the way.

She felt a snag on the top of her foot and found herself suddenly airborne, looking down at a patchwork of collapsed cornstalks. She landed hard on her shoulder with a sharp cry, curling up on top of the quilted stalks and holding herself in a hug as she absorbed the shock.

23

DALE KNELT at Odie's side, a gentle hand on her arm.

"What happened? Are you okay?"

"I tripped."

Odie's voice was laced with pain as she sat up gingerly, holding her shoulder. Her short hair had become unkempt, escaping the tacky pomade that kept it flat, the wind tickling the spikes.

She looked around, trying to find what it was that had sent her careening onto the hard ground. A cornstalk, neatly folded on its side, the only sign that it had been disturbed the slight dent where Odie's shoe had caught beneath it.

"Odie..."

Dale didn't have to say another word, for they had realized something was strange at the same time. The cornstalks were thatched neatly by fours, woven together like a basket, the pattern stretching out several yards in front of them. The perimeter was a circle with several paths shooting off in different directions, and those paths branching out into smaller tributaries, threaded all throughout the field. Odie couldn't tell if it was the ground that was singing with electricity or if it was just the adrenaline flooding her veins as she staggered to her feet, still holding her shoulder.

"It's a crop circle..." she said slowly, testing the sound of it on her tongue. "I heard about these popping up everywhere on the radio, all over the South. One in Alabama, another in Missouri. Even New Orleans."

"It has to be a hoax, right? It's always a hoax."

Odie shrugged, then hissed in pain at the movement of her shoulder.

"I don't know, but I don't think anyone knows it's here, at least not yet. I haven't heard anything about it, and it's too close to home."

"Probably some meth-heads."

"Ultra-coordinated, meticulously organized meth-heads?"

"Alright, you've made your point." Dale laughed, though Odie knew when Dale was uneasy. "We should—"

A sound loud as a crack of lightning reverberated across the field, the echo of it rushing off into the distance. A scream pealed out of Odie, her heart swelling in her throat as she grabbed Dale's arm and began running back in the direction of the car.

"Daddy!" she yelled, terror lighting up every nerve inside her, running almost through the corn paths. "Daddy! Bubba!"

Another shotgun blast, and somewhere far away a cluster of corn plants erupted into the sky.

"Oh my god." Dale's voice was quiet, trembling. "Oh, Jesus Christ, we're gonna die out here."

Odie saw the car ahead, could just make out her father and brother inside. Daddy was hanging out the door, screaming for Odie. Odie's ears, with the river of blood rushing through her head, couldn't hear a thing.

It was strange how she found herself suddenly inside the car with Dale, all the doors closed and the car fish-tailing onto the dirt road, the tires groaning angrily. A skip in time from the shock of it all.

"Faster!"

Dale hit the back of Daddy's seat, none of the bodies in the car still or settled. They were all cut electric wires whipping and sparking inside, all-consuming fear, a mess of energy like rabbits choking themselves in snares.

Daddy was going the opposite way from where they'd come, but he didn't have time to turn around and didn't have the mind to even if he wanted.

As the old car gathered speed, it began to slide across the gravel, the back tires whirring as plumes of dust enveloped them. Suddenly the car pitched sideways, the wheels disconnecting from the road as they spun. Daddy slammed on the brakes and all four of them were thrown forward as the car tilted into the ditch on the side of the road, the hood buried into the earth.

The car filled with a single long scream until the moment of impact, and then it was eerie-silent, dark soil thrown up onto the cracked windshield and slightly crumpled hood, jutting up on one side like a jagged tooth. Daddy was slumped forward over the steering wheel, Bubba curled against the dashboard, half in Daddy's lap. Dale's cheek was pressed into the back of Daddy's seat, and Odie had ended up in the floor somehow, looking up at Dale from below.

The inside roof of the car was a piece of thin fabric stretched over orange foam, where the nicotine smell of years and years of smoke clung, and it hung like a draped curtain in some parts, pinioned by sewing pins in a multi-colored constellation. It all swam in Odie's vision, the navy blue of the headliner darkening and the pins like swirling stars.

It took an eternity for Odie to remember to breathe.

24

2003

DALE'S WAS A BETTER house than Odie's, sat in the middle of a soybean farm so that the sky stretched over them like a planetarium on clear nights, the bottom of the sky *just* kissed by a row of trees. They took turns naming the constellations, giving their own names to the shapes. The Little Dipper was a Frog Leg and the Big Dipper was a Daddy Long Legs and Hercules was Sugar Loaf Mountain and on and on.

Dale's backyard was a strip of tangled wilderness that cut the soybean farm in two, and when they camped there at night they could hear the cracking of termite-bitten branches falling off onto the forest floor and imagined the crunch of raccoon feet ambling through the brush to be a Sasquatch or a werewolf and they giggled inside their tent with the flashlight trembling out at the darkness.

"It's the Blair Witch!" Dale would say, and Odie

would get very serious then and very scared and she would huddle against Dale until Dale would say, "If it *is* the Blair Witch, I'll protect you."

"I hope it's an alien," Odie would say.

"I don't. I don't want to get probed. Remember that movie *Fire In the Sky*?"

Odie would shudder. Yes, she remembered it. She wished she could forget. She didn't like to imagine aliens in that way, so cold, so indifferent to humanity, as if they were just fetal pigs in a silver dissection tray like she'd heard about from the junior high schoolers.

"I hope it's the kind of alien that's lonely. Just lonely and curious."

"I *would* like to hitch a ride with an alien to get out of Arkansas, even if it meant getting probed," Dale would say. "Only if it would let you come too."

"Only if it would probe just you," Odie would say, and they both would laugh, and Dale would agree to it, that she'd take the probing for Odie if it meant they could go somewhere far away together, like New York City, or maybe even another country. Someday.

25

ODIE SUCKED in a sharp breath and looked around, her neck aching.

"Dale?"

The inside of the car seemed to come slowly back to life. Bubba was righting himself in the passenger's seat while her father was wiping blood from his nose.

Odie felt a hand on her shoulder, pulling her up out of the floorboard.

"You okay?" Dale asked.

Odie could still hear that long scream in her head and realized now that it had been Dale's, and only then did the fear hit her heart like an arrow. Dale was okay, but Odie's body couldn't convince her that she was. Odie needed to touch Dale to know; she pulled herself against Dale and held her close, her fingers clutching at her back, both their hearts thrumming.

Once they were certain the farmer who had chased them off wasn't coming back, Odie, Daddy, and Bubba used their hands to dig the dirt out from around the car while Dale spun the wheels until it pulled free.

The car's lip was curled in a snarl, the headlights shattered. The ride back was silent until they turned down the dirt road that led to Odie's family's house.

"I really hope Denise took them oxys and passed out," Daddy said. "Otherwise she's about to kill me."

26

ODIE AND DALE WERE SHAKEN, but they didn't want to stick around for the inevitable fight that would break out between Daddy and Denise. Odie couldn't handle the shouting and shattering of glass, the slamming of doors and the scuffling that ended in loud sex. They decided to head to Little Rock, to the only gay club in the state.

27

2009

CLUB TRINITY SAT CRADLED in the heart of Arkansas. Sunday through Tuesday, it was a honky tonk, attracting cowboy-wannabes and women who still teased their hair into bleached blonde peaks on top of their leathery tanned heads. Students from the surrounding colleges got lit on Whiskey Wednesday and Thirsty Thursday, when the club became a rave. IDs were barely given a glance. On Fridays and Saturdays, Trinity became the only gay club in the state, its small stage playing host to drag acts, queens and kings, stiletto heels in a men's size 13.

The summer between high school and college, Dale and Odie spent a lot of time at Club Trinity, moving between the drag stage and the dance floor teeming with strobing lights that hit the black walls like confetti. They danced across Odie's face and lit up Dale's pale blue eyes. Their first time there together, Odie realized how pretty Dale was. It was one of the few things she remembered from that night.

Dale had been wearing a pair of cargo shorts and an oversized, sleeveless basketball jersey she'd had since middle school, and a pair of white sneakers she called her 'good shoes.' The ends of her hair were dyed dark, her long white-blonde roots strange under the black lights. Her haircut was lopped at the shoulders, one side flipping out while the other curled under her ear like a crooked smile. Odie noticed the way Dale's freckles swirled up her arm like a snake, and under the dancing lights it looked as if they too were dancing, a writhing constellation.

They were only 18, but Odie grabbed them both a Corona with lime from the bar by leaning over it and pulling her V-neck down just enough to draw the attention of the bartender wearing the bustier with the teased mohawk. The bartender had smirked knowingly, waving at Odie to put her boobs away before sliding the beers over to her and mouthing over the loud music, "Just one," and holding up one pointer finger for effect.

They drank their beers at the far perimeter of the drag stage because Odie was shy when the queens worked the crowd. She didn't like being drawn into their comedy routines; she couldn't give shade as well as she could receive it. Dale was the opposite, but happy just to be with Odie, to be laughing along.

When they threw their glass bottles out, they found themselves near the dance floor, which was empty save for a boy no older than 20, moving his limbs wildly in the corner as sweat dripped from his messy bowl cut.

Dale took Odie's hand and pulled her into the center of the room, pulled her close to her body and began rubbing against her as the music pulsed loudly against their skin. Odie remembered laughing, trying to make something silly out of something that felt more serious than she wanted to let on.

Her heart was beating fast, and faster every time Dale touched her. She put her arms on Dale's shoulders and tried to ride the wave of Dale's body as it rolled against hers, her head falling back as she looked up at the disco ball.

She watched it spin, a little tipsy from the one beer, Dale's sweat mingling in her clothes as their bodies traded warmth. When she looked up at Dale again, she was smiling at her, pulling her closer to kiss her soft lips, then Odie lowered her head to trace the freckles on Dale's shoulder with her tongue.

28

Baby

BABY SAW EVERYTHING. Baby wanted *that*. The memory playing in Odie's head was as crisp to Baby as it was to Odie. Baby heard music, faded and warbling like a warped record, and the beat like *rat-a-tat-rat-a-tat*. Thump thump thumping, the feeling of damp between Odie's thighs, a beating heart and rush of blood, swelling and sweating. *Rat-a-tat-tat.* Baby wanted that.

29

CLUB TRINITY HADN'T CHANGED. Standing in line in the cold, rough gravel parking lot, Odie looked around herself at all the variety, shapes and sizes of Southern queers, every shade and flavor, like peering into the freezer in an ice cream parlor.

Some of them looked like her brother, as if they were coming to see drag before an early morning hunting trip. They were decked out in camo and neon orange safety stripes that lit up bright in the black lights in the club. There were twinks and trans girls who'd borrowed their sisters' skirts and strappy wedge heels walking arm in arm with thick, big-breasted femmes with overlined red lips and winged eyeliner. There were sporty dykes like Dale and burly bears with rough hands and scattered gray in their chest hair peeking over mesh tank tops.

The Southern queers did not have the same air of self-importance as the queers in Massachusetts. If you were at Club Trinity, you were a poor gay, one who couldn't afford to go to a flashier club in one of the surrounding states, where they had actual gay districts, not just a single building sitting at the center of a broad rural state. Odie felt more at home here, the separation of classes no longer creating a gulf between her and any other queer waiting at the bar. The warmth of the realization made her bump into Dale's side affectionately.

The club doors opened and once inside, Odie and Dale made a beeline to the bar, trying to get ahead of the rest of the crowd filing in and ahead of the music that would soon drown out their voices.

"Corona with lime, right?" Dale said, flashing a grin at Odie.

"You remembered," Odie said, putting both hands over her heart exaggeratedly.

They leaned against the bar waiting for their drinks, looking at each other. One of Odie's hands slipped down to her stomach, a feeling inside like a knot being tied.

"You alright?"

"Yeah," Odie said, "just a little stomach thing."

"You have the shits?"

"Gross. No, I don't have the shits. I'm just a little shook up from earlier. Goddamn, you're nasty."

"Nastier than you know."

Odie shook her head and turned her eyes to the stage.

"Do you know who's here tonight?"

"Starr Light is the headliner," the bartender cut in, handing them their beers with a fresh little slice of lime peeking out of the salted rim of their bottles, "and I saw Big Boned go backstage a few minutes ago."

"Thanks, doll," Dale said, taking their beers with a wink.

"Bartender's hot," she whispered in Odie's ear lowly.

Odie felt another twinge in her stomach, some kind of pain she didn't readily recognize. A stab of white-hot jealousy.

30

THE STAGE WASN'T REALLY a stage at all, just a small platform a few inches off the ground that had been painted black, then repainted and repainted over as it chipped and aged so it was now bumpy terrain for drag heels to navigate. The performance area was small and cramped close to the stage, mostly standing room only, though there was a gaggle of soft butches in neon trucker hats sitting in the floor in a half-moon shape at the base of the stage. Some RuPaul number played over the loudspeaker.

"See that girl there?" Dale pointed to one of the soft butches, the one with the shaggy mullet jutting out under her neon green Spencer's hat.

"Yeah? What about her?"

"Look again. That's Annie Doolittle."

"No fucking way," Odie said, squeezing her lime into the small mouth of her bottle before pushing it through the neck. "The Annie that said we were gay for each other in middle school?"

"The very same. That's her girlfriend next to her."

"Jesus. It really is true what they say about homophobes."

"Hey, Annie! Annie!" Dale began to shout and wave to get her attention.

Odie grabbed at her hands, trying to push her arms down and cover her mouth at the same time.

"Shhhh. Shut... up!"

Annie whipped her head around and found Dale and Odie in the crowd, eyebrows bushy where they had once been perfectly manicured arches. They were drawn angrily.

"It's *Andy* now."

"Sorry, yeah, Andy. Hey Andy, remember us? Odette and Dahlia?" Dale pointed at the top of Odie's head, overly animated.

"Yeah. So?"

"No reason. Just wanted to say welcome to *The Club*. Did a representative mail you a copy of the Gay Agenda yet?"

"I'm with my girl. Y'all get out of here now, before I take you outside," Andy said, putting down her beer and making like she was ready to stand.

Odie was red with embarrassment, moving to hide behind Dale just as Dale turned to shake with laughter.

"Andy, she don't mean nothing by it. She only had half a beer and already don't make any damn sense. Pay her no mind," Odie said, a hint of pleading in her voice.

"I thought about asking how that pussy tastes, but that might be frowned upon."

Dale was shaking with laugher as she was led away by Odie, pulling a little too forcefully at her arm.

"That'd be an understatement."

Odie shook her head and drew Dale to the back wall, which was lined with hard wooden stools. They could still see the stage, but they were hidden by a human wall of business college fags in pastel linen shorts.

The emcee for the evening was a drag king with a long beard, a flannel crop top, and daisy dukes by the name of Dick DyNasty. He swanned from backstage with a cordless mic in hand, the heels of his rhinestone-studded cowboy boots thumping heavily on the hollow platform.

"Are y'all ready for some good old fashioned Southern loving?" The crowd cheered, but Dick DyNasty wasn't satisfied. "I said, 'Are y'all ready for some good old fashioned Southern fucking?'"

The crowd erupted in response, drumming their hands on the high tops and stamping their feet.

"That's what I thought," Dick said with a coy little smile.

Odie heard a soft moan beside her, then quickly shuffled closer to Dale. Dale looked to see what Odie was running from; a hetero couple were sitting on a barstool against the back wall, the guy's jeans undone and the girl's dress hiked up.

"Damn, she's working him like a pole," Dale snickered.

"*...warming up the stage for Starr Light, the sacrilegious breakfast queen, Gloria In Eggshells She's Deo!*"

"Let's move closer to the front again," Odie said. "Annie be damned. If I wanted to see straight porn, I'd have stayed home on Tumblr all night."

"It's *Andy* now," Dale said, mimicking Andy's twisted expression and cloying voice.

"Right. Andy." Odie rolled her eyes. Not that she didn't care about Andy's newfound queerdom. Like, good for her. But giving her respect when she never gave her any left a sandpaper feeling on her tongue.

Odie and Dale pushed their way back through the crowd just as Gloria began shaking her ass to "Like A Virgin."

"It's always Madonna at these shows." Dale swigged her Corona, then tucked a two-dollar bill into Gloria's panties.

"Can you grab me another drink, Odie?" Dale's eyes were firmly on Gloria's ass. "I don't want to miss this."

"You just said you don't like Madonna."

"It's not Madonna I'm here for." Dale laughed and handed Odie a five-dollar bill. "Get me a shot of Wild Turkey. If it's more than five dollars, we fucking riot."

31

Baby

THE DISCO BALL spun its glittery web over the walls, the floor, the ceiling, like so many dazzling... dazzling...

Baby could not draw forth the word until they pulled it through the sieve of Odie's mind.

Dazzling stars.

Disco.

Images of bearded men in bell-bottomed jeans and women in studded jumpsuits, thin trails of sweat snaking down an ebony collarbone, afros filled with *stars*. What a peculiar way to move, to gyrate, to undulate hips and pelvic bones, smell of sex and joy.

Baby was brought back to the here and now by the sound of dubstep like a car accident, a mechanical scream and beat drop that only seemed to enhance the emptiness of the dance floor adjacent to the drag hall, the sadness of the disco ball spinning round and round above a place where disco had come to die.

32

ODIE WAS, for the first time, under Baby's complete control, eyes glazed and expression slack as Baby struggled to understand skin and muscle, bone and movement, and all the memories and imagination that lay within their host.

33

Baby

BABY WAS the lone dancer on the small disco floor, face tilted back to the spinning light above like so many stars on their skin, sweat already gathering in the hollow of their neck.

Odie's skin.

Odie's neck.

Baby moved like swirling galaxies. Baby moved like a satellite beacon that drew others in by the throat. Baby was smashed now between two sexless bodies, arms lifted over their head, reaching and reaching.

The music shot through Baby's legs, and suddenly they were in the air, jumping with the beat of the music, the twang of the electric guitar guiding Baby's hips. Arousal flushed through Baby's groin and thighs as the hands of their dancing companions explored the body Baby shared with Odie.

Baby leaned in close to the nearest neck, tongue

lapping out to catch the dripping sweat slithering past their dance partner's ear, Baby's fingers pulling braided hair to the side to explore the taste of more skin.

Baby imagined sequined capes, glittered cheeks, large, doll-like lashes, bare chests. Baby felt as if their middle might burst, the bass tone of the disco-singer's voice like a thrum, thrum, thrumming of a humming tongue against Baby's most tenderest, swollen part.

Baby closed their eyes.

Baby inhaled the musk of their sin.

34

THERE WAS a sharp yank on Odie's arm. It pulled her back into herself. She was a stretched rubber band snapping back into place. Her breath heaved as if waking up from a dream, her hands grasping at the arm grasping her.

"Where the fuck did you go?"

It was Dale, her pale face looking even paler on the dance floor. The disco ball above was no longer spinning and the fluorescent lights had been flipped on, revealing the club to be the repurposed warehouse it really was. The music had stopped, and the only sound in the building was the drunken murmuring of tired queers filing out of Club Trinity.

Odie could only vaguely remember the heat of the bodies she'd been pinioned between, the way their sweat melted and mingled through the thin fabric of her shirt.

"I... I don't know," she said softly as Dale pulled her up the stairs that led away from the dance floor.

"You fucking disappeared! I was scared to death something had happened!"

"I'm sorry, Dale. I just... blacked out or something."

"You blacked out? Do you think someone roofied your beer?"

"I don't know. Maybe. I don't think anything bad happened, I just remember dancing."

And the feeling. A discomforting, strange feeling of being outside her body, or rather inside it and without control. It was like the first time she'd tried whippets, her head like a balloon on a ribbon above her body, her voice, her laughter in her ears as if it were coming through a can on a string.

Odie's temples throbbed as she was pulled out into the cool air.

"Slow down, Dale. My head's killing me. I'm sorry if I scared you."

"I'm pissed at you," Dale said, opening the door for Odie. "I'm pissed because I love you, and you *did* scare me."

For the first time, Odie realized Dale was shaking.

35

HER TEMPLES THROBBED with every pump of her heart. The music from Club Trinity still thumped inside her, the carousel in her head leaving her dizzy and covered in cold sweat.

Odie pushed her shades up her nose and hugged herself in her hoodie as Dale drove. The little hatchback rocked from side to side over the gravel road leading up to the Tucker house.

"Stop shaking the car."

"Stop living out in the boonies, then."

Dale was nursing her own hangover, squinting as she hunched over the steering wheel, gravel skidding under the tires. "I think the po-po is at your house."

Odie sat up gingerly, squinting through the trees as they rounded the corner to the lopsided house. Odie could see Daddy waving his arms, Denise's hands on his shoulders, trying to hold him back.

His voice cut through the thrumming in her ears, but the sound was unintelligible, muted by distance.

The cop's voice was a placating mumble, his hand extended the way a handler might try to placate a dog. The other hand was on his gun.

"Drive faster," Odie said as they made the final turn up the drive.

Had Daddy and Denise really gotten into that bad of a fight? They'd had the cops called on them before, for raising their voices, for breaking things. Denise once threw a lamp at Daddy and cut his elbow real bad. Daddy also had a few DUIs on his record, and Denise had done time on drug charges. A million different scenarios ran through Odie's mind.

Dale took a sharp turn into the grass to avoid the police cruiser, the hatchback lurching down, then bumping up over a shallow ditch. Odie was halfway out the door already, dropping to her knees in the grass. Everyone turned to look at her as she lifted her stained knees and approached. The cop's knuckles whitened over his side arm.

"That's my daughter!" Daddy shuffled quickly into the cop's line of sight again. "Don't you dare pull that gun, you son-of-a-bitch!"

Odie held her hands up. A growl rumbled from her belly, an ache throbbing into her nervous system that made her nearly drop to her knees again.

This was not a growl of hunger.

This was a wolf pawing at meat through a pane of glass.

"I'm Odette Tucker. I just want to know what's going on," she said tightly. She realized who was missing. "Where's Bubba? What's happened?"

"...and I'm Dale. Um, I'm Odie's friend. I'm not a threat. Please don't shoot me, *Mister Officer Sir.*" Dale stood beside Odie with her hands raised, the smirk on her lips offsetting the deep hatred in her eyes.

"My name is Sheriff Alcott. I come from Osceola to let y'all know Daniel Tucker's at Thompson Hospital."

"What for?"

Odie looked to Daddy. Panic was climbing up her throat, the tumult in her stomach like a roar. She could sense how no one wanted to say, could see the way the dark blue eyeliner ringing Denise's eyes had smudged, the mascara tracks down her sun-freckled cheeks.

"They hurt Bubba bad," Daddy said, his cheeks puffy, eyes bloodshot from rageful tears. "Them damn *pigs* shot my boy."

Bubba

NOW I AIN'T GONNA LIE, I was drivin' with a broke taillight.

If they told me that was a shootable offense, I wouldn't'a left the house. I done my time in juvie already, and the judge said if I caught another charge, I'd do adult time in an adult prison because I'm close enough to eighteen, and because I ain't been nothin' but a Hell-raiser since the day I turned twelve.

So I ain't no angel, and I'll cop to it, and I'll be damned if I ain't a little proud of it.

I knew it was wrong to go out with a broke taillight, but they was racin' cars out in Osceola, back on one of them dirt roads that hardly gets used except for if you're tryin' to get to a fishin' hole, and there was a buddy of mine out there that said he might need some backup. Not like we were anticipatin' a fight or nothin, but he'd got in trouble a couple times for sleepin' with some dude's old lady, and he didn't know if the guy was gonna be there or not. It was better safe than sorry, but I told him I wasn't gonna bring a gun, and I didn't. *I swear.*

When I saw the cop with his flashers in my rearview, I slowed down and pulled off to the side of the road right away. I didn't fight it or argue or nothin', just did what I knew was right to do, and sat there while his engine idled behind my truck.

The problem was my truck is a piece of shit. When I turn off the engine, it rolls backwards, especially if I happen to be on an incline like I was that night. It's why I always keep a brick under my seat.

I didn't want my truck stuck in some muddy ditch out in Osceola on top of whatever charge I was about to catch, so I took the brick out from under my seat and hopped out the truck as quick as I could, trotting to the back tire in a hurry.

It wasn't two damn seconds before I felt like I been hit with a baseball bat. I was layin' flat on my back, looking up at the stars, which were plenty that night. I heard a shufflin' of feet in the gravel and tasted dust at the back of my throat.

I could hear myself breathin' real heavy, and I wanted to ask about what the hell was goin' on, but when I opened my mouth nothin' came out. That's when it really hit me somethin' was wrong.

I could hear the police talkin' 'bout something while I lay there, but I couldn't make out the words. It all felt so far away from me at that moment, but I can tell you one thing, they was scared shitless.

I started to move a little, the heels of my boots scuffing at the gravel. I lifted my hand to my neck and it came away with blood. Then I pressed my palm back to the wound, which was still bleeding life itself.

I realized then I been shot in the neck. The brick still lay in one of my hands, and the truck had rolled into the ditch, the tailgate sunk in the mud and the front two wheels rearing like a horse.

The officer wouldn't get close to me, even though I was reaching for him with my free hand. I couldn't say anything, so I tried to beg with my eyes, but I couldn't see nothin' after a while and every thought I had felt like it was moving through swamp clay. Then there was no light at all, no movement, no sound.

It took me the longest time to realize they'd just up and left me there to die.

I was alone.

PART 2
PREPARE TO MEET GOD

37

THERE WAS NO THANKSGIVING.

Odie took a leave of absence from school for the rest of the semester, and Arkansas stretched out before her like a looming shadow, an expanse of cursed time with no end.

The longer she stayed, the more she became part of the land, melting back into its embrace, into the familiar patterns, into the strange stasis that settled over everything and everyone and made her feel as if she were locked in forever.

38

THE SAWMILL STOOD like the ruins of a country colosseum against the backdrop of a purple night. The dirt road caused Odie's car to sway from side to side, sliding over the dry gravel as the wheels kicked up plumes of dust.

It was a hot night for November. She was wearing an old T-shirt she'd found in one of the plastic bins in her room. The front was decorated with iron-on vinyl fan art of Kirk and Spock huddled in a loving embrace, which she'd printed off DeviantArt sometime in high school. It was threadbare now, worn down so thin her beige armpit-stained bra was showing through it, Kirk's face without definition like static on a box TV, and Spock's face erased altogether, leaving only a pointy ear and the back of his bowl cut. She was suddenly self-conscious.

She hadn't seen Dwayne in a long time, but she was happy that he asked her to come out to the mill after all that had happened, even if it was out of pity. She knew him well enough to know he wasn't exploiting her vulnerability, and yet the thought of him made her wet and wetter still as she neared the building.

39

2008

THE FIRST TIME Odie and Dwayne were in bed together, all hands, groping each other's bodies, he touched her soft belly. She tensed up like a cat, rolling away from him until he caught her by the hips and pulled her close again.

They kissed, Odie's hands sliding over the tufts of hair on his chest, down the furry line of his belly. She pulled at the worn leather of his belt. He hissed softly, whispering, "I can't."

"Why not? I want to." Odie tugged his belt again, as if to prove it.

"I know, and I do too. But I really can't."

"Is it me?"

"I'm afraid I'll hurt you. I'm—"

"'A vampire, Bella'?" Odie laughed at her own joke, but even in the dark she could tell he didn't get it.

"I'm too big."

Odie was glad of the darkness then. She let out a short laugh, but sensing the seriousness of the situation, her expression shifted to one of disbelief, balking.

"Are you joking?"

"No, I'm not joking," Dwayne said, tensing. "It's happened before, and I never want it to happen like that again."

"You hurt someone?"

"Not on purpose."

"Can I see it?"

"You can see it, touch it, play with it. I just can't, you know, put it in."

Odie reached out to touch and prod through his jeans, rubbing over the half-mast bulge straining against the worn denim.

"It's not so bad."

He reached down to free himself from the confines of his zipper. His cock sprang against Odie's hand, shaft filling hot with a rush of blood that inflated him until her fingers could no longer close around it.

"Jesus Christ. I thought this was just a thing guys said, about their dicks being too big."

"It is a thing guys say, but in this case…"

He nudged his hips up to rub the soft skin of his shaft against her palm, sighing softy like a dog at the pound who hadn't been touched in so very long.

"Is this okay," he whispered, lifting his hips again.

"Yes," she said, moving her hand along his length, pinning it down to see if it reached his knee—it touched his kneecap—then letting it spring back up against his fuzzy belly.

"Do you think it's weird?"

"I think it's amazing."

She played with it until he came.

40

WHEN ODIE first told Dale about it, in true Dale fashion, she'd nicknamed him Big Dick Dwayne.

"Don't say Big Dick Dwayne. Don't say Big Dick Dwayne. Don't say Big Dick Dwayne," Odie muttered to herself now as she pulled up beside a pickup truck.

From the old mill, Odie could hear an old radio blasting inside the tin shell of the abandoned warehouse, reverberating within the hollow of its gutted walls. She could see the silhouette of someone standing in one of the intact doorways, the red cherry of a cigarette glowing from inside a cloud of smoke. She parked next to a rag-tag cluster of old cars and pickups, just barely making out the curly mop of hair that was Dwayne's within the smoke's halo. His arms dropped out of the doorway, cigarette crooked in his mouth.

"Odette!"

He broke out in a light jog, covering the short distance, insistent on opening Odie's car door before she could even cut the engine. She opened it just as the car shuddered off. He dropped his hand away from the door as it swung.

"Beat me to it."

"Chivalrous of you."

She climbed from the car, allowing him to shut it behind her before wrapping him in a hug.

"How's Bubba?" Dwayne rubbed Odie's back, then pulled away to look her in the eye. "Still sleeping?"

"Still sleeping," she said, another blanket of heaviness settling on her chest.

"Any word on when he'll wake up?"

Odie shook her head.

"What about the cops that did this?"

"They're still on paid leave. Briggs is the name of the piece of shit that actually done it. Pulled the trigger. Alcott's the sheriff who told him to leave the scene, then made him come clean about what happened after the fact. If you ask me, they both did it."

"Them bastards. Are there gonna be charges brought?"

"Right now the only person with charges is Bubba. They're saying he came at Briggs with a brick. It's why he got spooked and opened fire." Odie folded her bare arms over her chest, looking at the ground and scuffing the grass with her shoe. "Do you have anything to drink in there?"

"Lots." Dwayne grinned and took her elbow, leading her through the old mill's doorway.

Inside, the sawmill was mostly empty, the equipment from its heyday gutted from the interior. In the center of the room there was a steel pallet stacked with sawn logs, layered similarly to the Lincoln Logs Odie remembered playing with as a kid. A few people she didn't recognize were sitting on top of the logs, liquor bottles glittering in the dim light of the battery-powered lanterns positioned around the warehouse.

She kicked at crushed beer cans as she walked, avoiding the scattered clear, green, brown glass of bygone bottles.

"Hey, guys, this is Odie," Dwayne said as he approached.

There were three boys, all around Odie's age. Two of them sat side by side, one forearm pressed to the other's with a lit cigarette in the crevice formed by their skin. Odie had seen this game before, when Daddy made Bubba play it with him. It was one of endurance, of pain tolerance. The cigarette melted away their skin as it sat between their arms, and whoever jerked away first was a pussy.

"Isn't 'Odie' that dog from Garfield," the unoccupied boy guffawed.

"Yeah, I've never heard that one before. That moonshine there?"

"Made it myself," Dwayne said, grabbing up the mason jar. The liquid inside was crystal clear, clearer than water, clearer than a pane of glass. "Want some?"

Odie took the jar up and opened it, taking a whiff.

"That'll melt the hair out your nose," Dwayne warned with a grin, proud of his creation.

The two boys facing off with the cigarette suddenly pulled apart, the cigarette falling to the ground. Odie stamped it out before taking a long swig from the mason jar. The mill filled with the excited howls of the boys.

"What? You've never seen a girl drink moonshine straight? I don't fuck with girly drinks."

Odie didn't know why she said it. Something about being steeped in so much testosterone, surrounded by the industrial smell of oil and wood shavings, emboldened whatever part of her that still hated being called a girl.

"No one but our mommas," replied one of the boys, his straw-like hair fanned out across his pockmarked forehead. "Sheee-it, that cigarette got me good."

"Pour some moonshine on it! Disinfect it 'n shit." The shorter of the three grabbed the jar from Odie and splashed some of the alcohol over the wound. Straw Boy yowled and danced away from the lumber pile, wringing his arm out.

"Goddamn it, Trash! Goddamn, that stings!"

Trash, the short one, doubled over in a fit of laughter.

"Your name's Trash?" She took the jar from Trash's hand, freeing it up so he could slap his knees. "I don't want to hear shit about my name being Odie then."

"My Pappaw nicknamed me that because I liked to play in his burn pile."

"With what little I know about you, that seems about right."

Dwayne laughed, draping his arm over Odie's shoulders.

"Let's start a fire. Trash, Lou, grab some of them logs

and pull them outside. Smells like oil in here. We wouldn't want to light the place up."

Lou was the quieter of the three. He got to work right away.

Odie let Dwayne steer her back outside. The surrounding field was flat, the dirt dry and cracked. Not even the weeds survived whatever made the soil turn sour. Trash and Lou hefted one of the larger logs between them, Straw Boy gathering up scattered dry wood and splintered log chips from the cement floor. The procession marched outside, through the field, to a cluster of trees that bordered the expanse of abandoned land. Through the foliage veil, down a steep, rocky embankment, Trash and Lou dropped the heavy log, letting their asses fall back in the damp dirt.

"I didn't know the river ran through here."

Odie helped gather up heavy rocks, the dark embankment lit only by the glow of a single lantern, which was held aloft by Dwayne until he found a low hanging tree branch to hang it on. She heaved and dragged the rocks into a tight circle, where Straw Boy and Dwayne began to teepee wood.

"You sure we won't get caught?"

"No way. Not many people know about this spot."

It took a while to coax the fire from an ember to a flame. Trash had gone back for the liquor, and they all sat around the fire, warming themselves with corn whiskey and talking about impossible futures.

41

Baby

BABY LISTENED IDLY TO THE BOYS' chatter at the fire. Odie filled herself with swig after swig of alcohol. Baby could feel it burning through her sinuses. Odie's fingers loosened around a mason jar, and Baby's fingers gripped it in turn.

"I need to stretch my legs. Wanna walk?" Dwayne asked Odie, standing and stretching his arms up to the moonless sky.

"Yes," replied Baby, rising on Odie's rubbery legs.

Baby liked this feeling, this strange, swaying feeling, like the wind had the body swaddled, cradled, shivering like tall grass. Baby stretched their arms too, gave a loud yawn, shook out the limbs, nearly fell into Dwayne.

"Careful!" He laughed, setting Baby right again. Dwayne's body was so warm, warm as the womb. Baby leaned in now, but Dwayne pulled himself away, taking

Baby's hand instead and pulling them up the rocky embankment.

Baby moved like a stumbling fawn over the clumps of dirt in the field. It appeared rock hard and cracked from drought, but with each step, their feet sank into the craggy soil. Baby gripped Dwayne's elbow, looking up at the dark sky. There it was, the thumbnail moon, blocked by the trees near the river, now smiling down at them like the Cheshire Cat.

The sky was pulsing, ripples of light emanating from the Cheshire grin as it turned into a frown. Dwayne didn't seem to notice, heading toward the parked cars outside the sawmill. He lay back on the hood, and Baby joined him, atop his body with thighs straddled over Dwayne's hips.

"Whoa," he said, smiling up at Baby. "What's this?"

Baby dipped down to kiss and suck at Dwayne's neck, tasting the Arkansas soil in his sweat.

"What are you doing?" He huffed and tugged at the back of Odie's shirt, but he was lifting his hips, his own shirt riding up on his pale belly. Baby saw the fur trail under his belly button and ducked to kiss that too, inhaling sharply. Then his lips now, parting them with Odie's tongue, exploring his mouth, the sharp, sweet taste of alcohol and cola, bitter taste of cigarettes.

Baby's fingers fumbled at Dwayne's zipper, unleashing his hardened cock, which bobbed and lay across his belly. Baby licked the trail of veins on his length, and Dwayne sighed, his blue eyes rolling up to look at the sky.

"The sky's moving," he muttered through gasping

breaths, slurping, sucking sounds smacking from his groin. "Odette…"

The Cheshire moon was somersaulting in slow motion across the sky, greens and blues ebbing across the dense black. The silver moon smiled, smirked, frowned, smiled again. It winked. A pulsing, whooshing sound filled both their ears, Baby's hands curling like claws into Dwayne's bony hips. Dwayne sat up suddenly, gripping Baby's shoulders and pulling them up.

"Hey, it's okay. You don't have to. We're drunk." His cock pulsed, dark with the tight swell of blood. He was leaking cum into the soft threads of his T-shirt.

"I want," Baby gasped, licking their lips. "But I want."

42

THE NEXT MORNING, Odie's head throbbed like a jackhammer, her jaw aching with tension.

She woke up on the hood of her own car next to Dwayne, who had wrapped her up in his jacket and arms to keep her warm. She could see her breath, it was so cold, their bodies covered in dew. The sawmill was shrouded in mist, fog over the damp, dead field. Odie sat up and Dwayne stirred, stretching until his arms trembled.

"Morning," he said, lifting himself up on his elbows.

"Did we...?" Odie brushed her short hair with her fingers, bringing her bangs back down over her eyes. They sprung up again, so she pushed her arms through Dwayne's jacket and put the hood on.

"What? Sleep together? You did get a little frisky, but I stopped you as soon as I could. I was drunk as a skunk." He sat up the rest of the way, rubbing the back of his neck with an aching wince. "A little mouth stuff, but I didn't let it get far."

"God. I'm really sorry. I can only remember bits and pieces…"

"It's okay, really. It happens." Dwayne patted Odie's knee, squeezing it before hopping off the hood.

"Where are the guys? Should we check by the river?"

"Wait a sec." Dwayne jogged lightly over to the mill, peeking his head in the doorway and calling out. When no answer came, he motioned for Odie to follow.

"They probably fell asleep by the fire. They couldn't have left, that's Trash's pickup and they all rode together."

They set out across the field again. The dirt had turned to a sticky clay in the morning mist, sucking at Odie's tennis shoes as they walked. She kept one hand on Dwayne's shoulder and the other on the trees they passed to help maintain her balance down the craggy embankment, down to the abandoned fire pit.

No one was there. Just the scatter of empty liquor bottles and a half-jar of moonshine sitting upright on top of a log.

"Maybe they went for a walk?"

Odie toed an empty whiskey bottle, listening to it scrape against pebbles.

"No tracks. Look." Dwayne pointed along their own footprints in the direction they'd just come. "Just ours. Nothing left from last night, even. Am I tripping or is that not weird as fuck?"

"They couldn't have just vanished. Maybe they were too drunk and decided to walk instead of drive."

Dwayne laughed.

"No way. Trash would drive, don't matter how drunk he was. All those boys have priors."

"What do we do? I have to get back. I have Bubba duty today."

Odie felt guilty for needing to leave, even if it was a good excuse. She didn't want to leave Dwayne holding the bag on a fucked-up situation.

"Go," he said, putting his hands on her shoulders. "I'll take care of this. They're probably doing some stupid shit out in the woods. I'll find them."

But Dwayne didn't find them.

No one ever would.

43

ODIE STOPPED by McDonalds for a black coffee on the way to the hospital.

The coffee was bitter, biting the back of her tongue and leaving her saliva sour in her mouth. But coffee was coffee, and she needed it no matter what it tasted like, if not for the pick-me-up then to wash the taste of dick and liquor from her teeth.

She swung by Dale's to pick her up on the way. It was a little over half an hour to the hospital Bubba had been airlifted to in Little Rock. Dale fed Odie a PB&J while she drove down the highway, thumbing jelly away from the corner of her mouth every now and then and sucking it from her thumb.

"Did you have fun with Big Dick Dwayne last night?" Dale was probing. Odie knew it, and Dale knew Odie knew it.

"I honestly don't remember much. There were some weird guys there. We split from them and fell asleep, and they were gone when we woke up. The whole night was a little weird."

Dale tore off another sloppy piece of sandwich and offered it to Odie's lips. She accepted.

"Did you drink too much?"

"Uh huh. They had moonshine."

"Shit. That stuff will get you fucked up. You'll end up like that guy Ray. You know, the one with the big baseball tumor in his cheek? All kinds of fucked up on that homemade stuff. His face is red as a beet from all the burst blood vessels."

"What makes you think that's all from moonshine?"

"Well, it prolly ain't, but you can't deny it could have played a role."

Dale laughed, and her laugh made Odie laugh. She silenced her with another bite of sandwich.

"Listen, bad shit can happen when you're drinking like that with a bunch of guys, especially guys you don't know. You need to be more careful."

Odie's chewing slowed. She didn't look at Dale, didn't look anywhere. Just kept her eyes on the road.

"I was with Dwayne. I trust him like family. He'd have put a boot up the ass of anyone who messed with me."

"Yeah, well Dwayne's about as big around as a pencil. His dick's bigger than he is."

"...You have a point." Usually Odie would laugh, but she didn't this time. "I was safe. I didn't feel unsafe, and if I did, I'd have gotten out of there, okay?"

"Sometimes I'm not so sure, Odette."

"What do you know about it?" Odie snapped.

"Dang, chill. I didn't mean nothing by it. I just want you to be safe, that's all. You been acting weird ever since you came home, disappearing at Trinity and now blacking out at a party in the middle of bum-fuck nowhere. You've always been a little self-destructive, but that kind of thing ain't like you."

Odie shrugged, keeping her eyes narrowed on the road, watching the yellow lines flash by like scars torn on the highway. The silence hung between them, the air feeling thicker, a little harder to take in. Odie realized it wasn't the air at all, but a tightening in her chest. She felt like she would scream, and the fear of screaming suddenly overcame her. A flash of heat followed by a chill ran through her, her forehead going ice cold and sweat drenching her palms.

"I need to pull over," Odie said suddenly, a tremble climbing her throat.

"What aren't you telling me?"

"I can't... I need to pull over *right now*, Dale. I'm freaking the fuck out. I need to pull over."

The car swerved onto the shoulder of the highway, tires skidding as Odie slammed on the brakes. They both lurched forward suddenly, then slammed back in their seats. Dale was clinging to the car door handle, lifted up out of her seat in alarm.

"Odie, what is it? Jesus Christ, you're scaring the shit out of me!"

"I'm scaring the shit out of myself. I can't breathe."

Odie opened the door and all but fell out, scrambling over the gravel to circle the car so that it hid her from the passing traffic. She sat down on the side of the road, drawing her knees up and putting her face in her hands. Her heart was pounding, pounding like a bludgeon, and the smaller she made herself, the more violent it felt.

Dale sat beside her, rubbing her back and saying nothing for the longest time. Her breathing slowly evened out, the tight muscles in her back relaxing. Air came easier and the cold blood inside ran warm again. She looked at Dale finally, tears clinging to her eyelashes like snowflakes.

"I ain't told nobody this," Odie whispered, "but something very bad happened to me."

44

Odie

I WAS RAPED. Don't get upset. I'm just trying to get it all out, let me get it all out before you lose it, okay? Bear with me now, because I haven't told a soul before this. I just didn't know how I could. I still don't.

This is how it happened.

You think it was easy moving so far away from home, but it wasn't. You think it was a ticket to somewhere better, but I've learned all places are about the same. There's good and bad to 'em, but mostly bad.

School was going okay, but it'd been a year, and I hadn't really made any friends. There were people I could hang out with, but it wasn't like us and Dwayne. I was missing y'all bad.

I have this roommate, Heather. She's kind of a goth, kind of a gutter-punk, a little like us in spirit, but she's heavy into drinking and drugging. Not the real hard stuff, but she'll try just about anything once. We aren't close or anything, but she found out I'd be alone on Halloween, so she invited me out with a few of her friends.

I didn't know any of them. I don't even remember their names now, if I'm being honest. We went to zombie laser tag, which is exactly what it sounds like. I had a lot of fun, but it was over by ten o'clock, and half our crew wasn't ready for the night to end.

We decided to go back to campus. There was a small Halloween party on the quad. It wasn't anything formal, just a group laying out on the grass sharing straight vodka and whiskey. I didn't know any of them, I think they were mostly freshman.

It kind of reminded me of home a little bit, even though we were in the middle of a city. This little patch of grass...

And anyway, we joined the group, and I started drinking, kind of showing off that I can drink whiskey straight and it's nothing to me *even though I'm a girl*. I don't know why I did that. It seems really stupid to me now, that I did that.

There was a guy there who said his name was Will. He was a freshman. He was a really pale guy with blond hair and blue eyes and really bad acne. I didn't think he was cute or anything. He really seemed like kind of a douche, kind of jock-y and like he thought he was smarter than everybody else. But he seemed interested in me, and we were all having a good time, so I thought, "Why not?"

Heather tried to get me to leave with her, but by that time I was so drunk I could hardly see straight. She ended up leaving me there on the quad because she was ready to go back to the dorm and pass out. I had already set my sights on going back to Will's place.

On the way over, I asked him if he had a condom, and he said he did. I made him show it to me. He pulled out his wallet, and there it was. I told him over and over on the walk there that this wasn't going to happen without a condom, and each time he said, "I know! I know."

I didn't feel safe with him, because he was a stranger, but I didn't feel unsafe either. Do you know what I mean?

He lived alone in one of those suites you can rent on campus, if your parents are rich enough to pay for it. There was a doorman and everything. I remember him giving us a look as I stumbled into the lobby, a knowing look, but he didn't stop us or ask us what we were up to. I was giggling madly.

The suite had white walls. It was dark when we entered it, and he never turned on the lights. I'm just realizing that now, that he never turned the lights on, not once.

He showed me where his bed was, and I asked him where the condom was. He said he'd lost it on the walk over.

I didn't believe him. He pulled out his wallet and pretended to look for it, then showed me. He said, "See? It's not there."

I told him nothing was gonna happen without it. That we could fool around a little, but we couldn't have sex without it. He seemed okay with that, so we got into bed.

We kissed and touched each other a little, but by that time, I was so sleepy-drunk, I wasn't even really into it anymore. I told him I just wanted to go to sleep.

I passed out.

45

Odie

WHEN I WOKE UP NEXT, he was on top of me. This is the part that's hardest to tell.

46

Odie

I FELT TRAPPED BENEATH HIM, not just by his body, but like I couldn't hardly move at all. My head was swimming from all the whiskey I drank. I think back on it now, I don't know how it didn't kill me, and sometimes I wish it had so I wouldn't have to live with the memory of what it was like to feel so helpless.

His hips were pressed between my legs, and I felt the hardness of him pushing against me, trying to pry me apart. I shoved my forearm against his chest, trying to hold him back, not to feel his sour breath on my neck.

My other hand went between my legs to try to block him. I kept saying, "No. No. No. No!"

I could barely feel my body. I felt weak. All I could think was that I couldn't believe this was happening, and I hoped that I wouldn't get pregnant from this.

I felt both his hands curl around my wrists. He

slammed them down above my head and held them there.

Then he raped me. I felt him inside me, could feel his hips rocking me, and then I just blacked out. It could have been because I was so drunk, but I think it was my mind's way of protecting me.

The next morning was the strangest morning I can ever remember. There was this sense that life would now and forever be divided between before and after this. Light came in through the windows, dull and gray. There was a blanket thrown over me, and he was sleeping beside me, like he wasn't a criminal, like he hadn't just done what he did.

I shook him awake. It felt like waking a dragon. I told him we needed to go right now, right now. I needed a ride to the drug store. I told him he was paying for half of my Plan B. I acted like I didn't know he'd raped me. I acted like I didn't know it had been wrong.

In the parking lot, I asked him his name again.

Then he said it was Ethan.

And I said, "I thought your name was Will?"

And he said, "It is Will. Just kidding! It's actually Greg. Or is it Will? Or is it Ethan? I'm sure you'd like to know!"

And he laughed at me.

47

Odie

I TOOK the Plan B in the car. I felt shaky. I realized I was scared. He prattled on and on about his brother being on the rowing team, how they were rowing the Charles River that day. His voice sounded far away, like a warbling broadcast on an old radio.

He pulled over on the street in Harvard Square, but he didn't unlock the door of the car. He said he was too busy that day to drive me all the way back to my dorm. He told me to give him my phone number. I was too afraid not to, so I did.

I moved to open the car door, but he stopped me. He told me to pull out my phone so he could see the screen. He dialed my number and watched it ring. He smiled.

He said, "I just wanted to make sure you didn't give me a fake number."

I got out of the car and walked through Harvard

Square. It was so cold, I could see my breath that morning. The cold was all I could feel.

It felt like the most intense walk of shame. I was in shock, and I felt dirty. I felt like I was wearing someone else's skin. I think it all showed in my face. I can only imagine what I looked like.

I remember this man passing me by. A gruff man with stubble on his chin and a thick Boston accent.

He said, "Smile, honey. It ain't *that* bad!"

That's when I realized I was still holding the Plan B box, crushed in my fist.

48

DALE WAS quiet for a long time after Odie finished speaking.

"Please say something."

"I don't know what to say," Dale said, "except that I'm so sorry you went through all that, and I wasn't there. Did you tell the police?"

"I almost did."

"Well, why didn't you? Why didn't you get the bastard?"

"I was scared to. When I went home, the first thing I did was take a long shower. I just wanted him off of me. Then I laid in the bed for two days straight before my roommate asked me what happened. She took me to the doctor, but she said it was too late for a rape kit because it'd been a few days, and I'd already showered."

"So you couldn't report it without the kit?"

Odie shrugged, and Dale's brows drew together tightly, the peaks of the wrinkles sharp as razorblades.

"So you *could* report it, and didn't?"

"The doctor told me if I was her daughter in this situation, she'd tell me not to report it. She said a trial would be more damaging to me than what had happened because there was no evidence from a rape kit, and they'd air all my dirty laundry to make me seem more unreliable than him. Like my mental health stuff and everything with my family being...well, the way that they are. And I didn't want that, Dale. I couldn't go through something like that."

"Christ," Dale said. "So you took Plan B?"

"And it didn't work."

"You mean...?"

"Yeah. It was less than a three percent chance, but Tuckers ain't never been lucky. I was pregnant. I had an abortion. It was early enough, I could do the pills. It happened on my drive home."

"You said you ain't told no one, but you told two people in Boston," Dale said softly, "and they did fuck-all about it."

"I didn't tell no one that really mattered, is all. But I'm telling you now."

Dale was quiet again. Odie studied her face, those ice-blue eyes that were now averted to knobby, thin knees. Odie was looking for Dale's judgment, for more insistence that Odie should have reported the rape anyway. For Dale to say that it was Odie's responsibility that she prevent this from happening to anyone else ever again.

But those words never came.

Baby

BABY HEARD IT ALL. Anger like heat. Anger building like volcano, like slaughtering lava burning up everything and everyone.

Baby let Odie sleep once she was back home, their joint body needing respite. Baby was studying Odie's dreaming mind. Intense rage and sorrow and fantasies of revenge percolating under the surface that Baby couldn't be sure belonged to Odie or itself.

Shotgun sound from an old Western. Explosion sound from a documentary. The dead soldier from down the road. The stray dog the neighbor shot. The Twin Towers falling down and down and bodies falling with them. Fear and chaos, and at the center of it all was everything bad that had ever happened to Odette Tucker. All of it, every bit of it, was connected.

Baby was learning a lot.

Baby

BABY WAS HOME ALONE. The lopsided house groaned and whistled as wind swept through the small clearing on which it sat.

Baby was standing in the mirror, looking at itself, at Odie's self, skin bare and olive. Baby touched Odie's breasts, cupping the weight of them and tipping them up and down like a scale trying to balance itself. The nipples were large and purple and pointed down to the floor when Baby let the breasts drop unsupported.

Baby's hands moved to the cunt between thick thighs, feeling the soft, dark hair there, pushing a finger between the furred lips and rubbing over the dry clitoris.

"Oh," Baby said, furrowing Odie's brows as they shifted their legs further apart.

Baby pushed a finger inside and wriggled it around, smiling. Oh, yes, Baby remembered this. Warm and wet. Comforting. So strange to be the egg and not the yolk.

Baby pulled the finger out and wiped the juices on its thigh, moving to Odie's suitcase now and unzipping it. Baby pulled out the bras and panties, the T-shirts and worn sweatpants and the Walmart hoodie with *Be Fearlessly You* emblazoned across the front. Baby tossed it all away with a *harrumph!*

Baby moved like a crab from Odie's bedroom, through the narrow doorways and the stained carpeted living room, into Daddy and Denise's bedroom. The air was heavy with the smell of weed and chewing tobacco. Empty, clear vodka bottles with red tops lined the windowsill above the bed and a floppy orange dildo was suctioned to the bedside table.

Baby pulled open a drawer and rifled through stained underwear and men's boxers, holding up a pair and stretching them. The fabric was so worn Baby could see right through them, and it made them giggle like a madman when they released the elastic and watched the boxers soar through the air, landing on top of the rubber dildo that shuddered under its weight.

Baby opened another drawer, pulling out wadded up and twisted lingerie in red, black, baby blue, and bright pink. They were tangled up in a ball of colors like yarn, and Baby worked to unknot them with fingers that were growing more dexterous the longer they occupied Odie's body. The red lingerie snapped free and Baby turned it over and over, trying to figure out which way was up and how such a thing fit on a human body. They pushed their fingers through the open crotch and wriggled them before dropping the stringy one-piece off to the side.

Baby freed a black mesh bra and skirt from the lingerie ball and pulled the top over Odie's breasts, lifting them into the see-through fabric. Then the skirt, which was no more than a stretchy strap of fabric that barely covered Odie's ass.

A wall mirror leaned against the nicotine-stained walls, coated in splatters of unknown origin, fragmenting Baby's reflection as they admired Odie's body in the mesh net. Baby stood like a starfish, stretching their arms up so the downward-pointing nipples hung out the bottom of the mesh, their legs open and testing the confines of the skirt.

Baby was feeling itself.

Odie, who had always hated the sight of her own breasts—nipples like dinner plates—an old boyfriend had once said, was feeling herself too from behind Baby's gaze, through her own eyes.

51

Baby

BABY DIDN'T KNOW how to drive, but Odie did.

Behind the wheel of Odie's speeding hatchback, the car's tires slid over the gravel precariously as Baby's bare foot pressed down on the pedal. It began to shift sideways going around a bend toward the main road, and Odie righted the car with a swift jerk of the wheel, gravel rumbling and kicking up with metallic tinks against the bottom of the car.

As the gravel gave way to asphalt, Baby's foot grew heavier on the gas. The engine groaned loud as a mountain lion, fast as one too, whipping down the empty highway at midnight toward Osceola and never letting up on the speed.

There were no lights, just blackness on either side of the road and long stretches of empty fields and cracked dirt. Occasionally a pickup truck full of workmen or messy-haired teenagers raged by, a fleeting blast of country music or AC/DC and raucous laughter rushing by, the sound warped by the speed, twisting into something otherworldly.

Baby made a beeline through the small town center of Osceola, a single stretch of paved road preserved in time like a mosquito in amber. The ice cream parlor and the gas station sat exactly where they had been constructed in 1946, the paint chipped and dirt bleeding down their white façades like blood in the moonlight. The courthouse was no bigger than the ice cream parlor, and the town jail was attached to the building, about the size of a double-wide trailer. Baby gunned it beside the jail, but all the cruisers parked there were empty and none followed the speeding car.

The town was completely silent and dark, save for a light at the end of the paved street. Sound came thumping from within a red-bricked building, the glass door propped open by a coffee can of cigarette ash. Red-faced men in uniform stood outside smoking and guzzling Bud.

Odie whipped the car into a spot beside the only police cruiser in the lot and together Odie and Baby watched and waited.

52

Baby

BRIGGS WAS GETTING sloshed and didn't stumble to his truck until an hour later, his companion helping him into the passenger's side.

"I'm fine, I'm fine, Alcott," Briggs slurred, his blue eyes spider-webbed with deep red vessels. "I can drive, damn it!"

"Think you've gotten in enough trouble this week. We can only handle one crisis at a time."

Alcott's voice hovered between serious and playful scolding, shutting Briggs's door before circling to the passenger's side.

Baby was standing there, leaning against the truck door, arms stretched up and behind her head, mesh stretched over bare skin, goose-pimpled in the cold.

"Jesus Christ," Alcott said, his hand moving to his firearm only briefly before dropping to his side. His tone shifted once he'd taken Odie's body in, eyes lingering at the bottom of her soft belly, interested now. "Where'd you come from?"

"We been waitin'," said Baby, fingers hooking in the waist of Alcott's pants, "for the two of you."

"Oh?" Alcott allowed her to fiddle with his button. "Do I know you?"

"Nope." Baby giggled. "Do ya want to?"

Baby lifted its arms again, stretching languidly as a cat, letting Odie's head drop back on the truck. Briggs could see the mesh-covered ass smooshed up against the window, his voice muffled as he howled.

"Let her in, Alcott! Don't be a faggot."

"Ain't no faggot, Briggs. Watch your mouth in front of the lady."

His hoppy breath was hot against Baby's neck, their legs wrapping around his waist as they clung to him like an armadillo. He unhooked her legs and pushed Baby back against Odie's car, chuckling.

"Eager little whore, aren't you? We can't do this here."

"I know a place a couple hours from here," Odie said. "All the privacy we could want, not a chance you'll be seen by anyone you know. Including your wife."

Odie's eyes dropped to Sheriff Alcott's wedding band, which had grown tight around his fat finger over the years.

"Shh, shh. I ain't married tonight." He pressed a finger to her lips. "Where is this place?"

"Out in the middle of nowhere, where no one can hear me scream," Baby said with a wicked little smile. "Follow my car, I'll show you."

53

Baby

IT WAS 3 a.m. by the time they arrived at the deserted sawmill, the only light the light coming from the beams of their cars. The truck followed behind Baby, the energy of the men within radiating against Odie's back as if they were stalking sharks. The hatchback squealed to a stop in the same tire grooves from the other night, when Odie had been parked there to party with Dwayne.

Alcott and Briggs climbed out of the pickup, leaving the headlights on to illuminate the old building. Briggs had sobered up some, his eyes and face a little less red and bloated, his gait less staggering.

"Damn, you weren't kidding," Alcott said, adjusting his balls through his britches. "What is this place?"

"An old sawmill," Odie-Baby said, slinking over to Alcott and taking his large paw in Odie's hand. Baby reached for Briggs's hand too, pulling them both toward the leaning door. The headlights provided just enough light to see by as they passed through, the dusty smell permeating their noses. Briggs sneezed and wiped a snotty nose against the back of his hand as both men were led to the lumber flat in the center of the room.

"You've been here before?" Briggs asked, nodding at the bottles littered everywhere, the gleaming jewels of shattered glass glittering in the dim light pushing past cracks in the façade.

"Once," said Baby.

"With a john?"

"With a Dwayne." Baby climbed up onto the lumber pile, laying on their back and spreading their legs to show off what lay between.

Alcott did not wait for a conversation with Briggs regarding the etiquette of who got to go first. Alcott's superior rank made him the alpha and Briggs his cuck. He unbuckled his trousers and let them slip just below his lily white and red-pimpled ass, pushing himself between Odie's legs with a grunt. His cock was small and shriveled, even when it was hard inside a soft pussy. Baby could barely feel it as he began a rut, punctuated by effortful grunts; his sex was artless and wholly self-serving, face swelling with huffs and puffs of stinking breath in Odie's face. He lasted less than two minutes, pulling out and coating Odie's thighs and belly in cum, a horned-up look in his eye like a dog breeding a bitch.

Baby laughed, stretching, pressing a bare foot to the center of Alcott's chest to push him away.

"His turn," Baby said, holding out their hands

toward Briggs and opening and closing their fingers into fists. Grabby hands.

Briggs was eager when he saw Baby's eagerness, though he stopped short of putting his dick in when he saw the amount of Alcott's cum pasted over their skin.

He shed the top of his police uniform, the buttons and badges clattering to the floor in a heavy heap. Then he pulled the white tank top over his head, using it to mop off Alcott's cum and tossing it away like an old oil rag.

Baby hooked their legs around Briggs's waist then, sitting up and draping their arms around his neck as he pushed inside with a groan. He pumped his hips as Baby rode the force of his cock, sighing softly into his ear. He gripped Odie's thighs and lifted her to smack her ass, tearing at the mesh lingerie, teeth biting into her cold skin. Baby let out another exaggerated moan, head lolling back, rolling to look at the little row of shiny whiskey bottles on top of the lumber flat.

"I gotta take a leak," Alcott said in the dark background, moving outside with his trousers still open, expecting another round. Neither Briggs nor Baby responded, the sounds of their sighing and grunts dampened in the moist hollow of the old mill.

Baby reached back, curling their fist around the neck of one of the whiskey bottles.

"Wait, no," Odie whispered to Baby.

"No, no. Not now," Briggs said, holding her hips bruisingly tight and pumping harder, "I'm close."

"...Do it," Odie said, releasing the rigidity in her arm.

Baby swung the bottle, the thick glass colliding with

Briggs's head. The bottle against skull made a sound almost like a wine cork popping. It wasn't like in the movies, where it shatters on the first try. Briggs staggered back as Baby slipped off the lumber, leaving scrapes and splinters in Odie's ass and thighs.

"Christ!" Briggs roared, stumbling back, then forward, his hands out and tensed as if they were already around Odie's throat.

Baby swung the bottle again, this time against Briggs's jaw. It shattered this time, shards like diamonds embedding into his jaw as it broke into a sideways grin. He screamed as it flopped open limply, his tongue hanging out, drooling blood that dripped down his chest and tinkled across the floor. He staggered again, reaching for his gun just as Baby ran toward him, the sharp neck of the bottle wielded like a dagger, and embedded that dagger into the soft jelly tissue of his eye socket.

Alcott burst through the door, lopsided as Briggs's jaw, panting with his dick still out. Briggs was staggering around like a zombie, batting at his eye. Baby was nowhere to be seen, and the gun at Briggs's hip was gone from its holster.

"Briggs!" Alcott shouted, sprinting to the wounded deputy.

His remaining eye had a dead stare, his hanging jaw flapping as wildly as his flailing hands, spewing blood across Alcott's face as he tried to still the stumbling man.

"Hold still, man. Jesus Christ!"

He gripped the neck of the bottle and pulled it free

of Briggs's eye socket with a squelch; the glass just seemed to keep coming and coming, the large shard jagged. Briggs went quiet and still before Alcott, the hole in the socket squirting blood with every hard pump of his heart. Then the remaining eye rolled back and he dropped hard as a stone at Alcott's feet, his legs and hands twitching as his body seized.

"You bitch!" Alcott snarled, throwing the bloodied bottle neck away from him and drawing the gun on his hip. He backed up against the nearest wall, then worked his way around it, his frantic eyes bulging from his sweaty face.

His gun whipped in the direction of every creak and groan the old mill made, the wind outside causing the tin roof to whistle a quiet, eerie little tune before wailing and chattering like a banshee when the gusts across the plains pushed in a new direction.

"Where are ya?" Alcott growled and turned quickly at the sound of skittering footsteps, firing his weapon like the sound of thunder.

A piercing squeal, the light catching the black eyes of a possum as it scuttled and cried, leaving a dark trail of blood across the concrete. He fired again and the possum's belly popped like a bloodied grape, the fat body leaping into the air and landing in a quiet heap.

Baby watched all this from a crouch in the darkest corner of the wide warehouse floor, where the beam from the headlights outside couldn't reach. Both of Baby's hands gripped Briggs's gun as they duckwalked along the perimeter of the space in a deep, crab-like squat. When Alcott turned his back to Baby at the rustling of loose brush outside scraping the side of the building, Baby stood up behind him and pressed the Glock to the back of his neck.

Alcott froze, releasing his firing stance and moving his hands up beside his head very slowly, his neck burning red.

"What's this about?" He asked through gritted teeth as Baby took his gun from his clenched hand.

"Turn around," Odie said quietly, her voice trembling from rage. "I want to know what happened to Daniel Tucker."

"Is that what all this is about? The boy assaulted a police offic—"

The bullet left the gun like the crack of a whip, taking off Alcott's first three toes inside his snakeskin boots. He yowled and fell back on his ass, leaving a trail of blood as he scooted to put his back against the pile of lumber, holding his foot and cursing loudly.

"You goddamn bitch! You two-timing, whoring, murdering Jezebel!"

"Are you finished?" Odie watched Alcott with all of Baby's indifference to his suffering, the fired gun warm in her hand. "Tell me what happened the night Daniel Tucker was shot. Tell me what *really* happened or the next thing I shoot won't be your foot."

Alcott panted, pale, taking off his boot and sock and watching the disembodied, flesh-and-bone remains of his three toes slop onto the floor. He wailed again, wrapping his sock tightly over the wound and pulling it with a cry.

"I told the truth in my report. He had a busted taillight. Briggs pulled him over, and he went at my deputy with a brick. He had no choice but to shoot. The rookie panicked, no doubt about that, but the Tucker boy is to blame. That's all there is to it."

"No, that's not all," Odie said, pointing the gun between Alcott's legs.

"Wait, wait!" He gasped, now eager to tell more, panting like a dog. "Briggs left him there. Called me. I'm the one who convinced him to fess up. If it weren't for me, Tucker would still be laying on the side of the road. You should be *thanking* me."

Odie laughed through Baby, or was it Baby laughing through Odie? In this moment, they were one and the same, their consciousnesses fused. Odie's body and Baby's inhibition. A monster. An angel. Something more powerful than either of those things.

Alcott said nothing, his bulging eyes glowering at Odie. Baby crouched, pressing the gun up under the flap of Alcott's fat chin.

"The boy survived. I don't know what more you want from me," Alcott said, gruff voice trembling, fearful. "He's alive, ain't he? Well, ain't he? I got a wife. I got three kids."

"Shhhhh," Baby whispered, putting their finger over Alcott's blubbering lips, tilting their head to one side, then the other.

"Why do you care about someone like Daniel Tucker? Who are you?"

Odie smiled.

"I'm his sister."

54

Baby

BABY FIRED THE GUN, the top of Alcott's head spitting like a geyser.

55

WHEN ODIE OPENED HER EYES, the inside of the warehouse was turning gray with dawn. Her arms and legs felt numb from cold, and when she moved the dried blood on her skin crackled like old paint.

She heard a snuffling, skittering sound, her eyes shifting to the bodies of Briggs and Alcott. There, a trio of armadillos had begun to pick apart the flesh, their scaled paws scratching at the cement floor as they braced themselves, pulling meat and sinew from tendon and bone. Briggs's face was already gone, his skeleton grinning bloodily up at the ceiling, while Alcott's brains were snuffled and slurped from the floor by a possum that had joined the armored band.

Odie got to her feet shakily, her blood-soaked hair hanging in spikes over her eyes as she walked, shoulders hunched and legs trembling, toward the door with the Glock still clutched in her hand.

She stumbled barefoot toward the steep embankment that led down to the river, the sharp rocks jutting out of the dirt scraping at the bottoms of her feet. She waded into the icy water, the current gentle as the sun broke through the blade-like branches of the barren trees.

She stopped when the water lapped at her hips, pulling her arm back and launching the gun into the deeper waters at the center of the river. A swirl appeared on the surface of the water, a whirlpool sucking the Glock down into the cloudy depths, laid to rest among the catfish and mudpuppies.

She lifted her chin to the sun, closing her eyes, her heart pounding in her chest and ears. What had she done? It had seemed right in the moment, but now? Now there were two dead cops and a police cruiser she had no idea what to do with. The dead leaves in the forest rustled with bottom-feeding life, a scattering of birdsong cutting through the silence.

She didn't think of her family, what they might think of all this if she were discovered, nor did her thoughts turn to death row, final meals, and fist fights in isolated cell blocks. Instead, she thought of everything she had worked to achieve; her academic scholarship, dorm life and a reliable bed and three cafeteria meals a day, honors classes and the hope she had hung on her degree ever since she could remember. Daddy always said that a good education was her ticket out of the life her family had lived for generations, a life of blood and sweat and soil.

But it didn't matter where in the world she went, this life followed, nipping at her heels like a wild dog.

56

ODIE SAT on the wet shoreline of the river, squishing her toes in the mud, pulling them up and listening to the suckling sound of the earth trying to pull her back down. She wasn't sure how much time had passed when she realized her hair had dried, wafting in the breeze like a soft curtain against her temples.

She gathered herself up and shook the mud from her toes, dipping each foot in the water and peddling them up and down until the muck cleared from her skin, leaving just a dark crescent moon beneath her toenails. Then she scrambled back up the embankment, tearing at roots and carefully avoiding the poison ivy clawing at her ankles.

She trudged back across the field, an arm wrapped over her breasts, the warmth of the sun a stinging kiss on her bare skin.

When Odie reached her car, she pawed the inside of the glove compartment for her cell phone. It was off, and there wouldn't be any signal so far out. She'd have to drive in closer to town.

She cast a wary glance at Briggs's truck, then at the crooked mouth of the mill's entrance. She could see the shadows of vermin scuttling in the shrouded darkness within, and a snake winding its way through the doorway to join them.

She climbed into her car, turned the ignition, and rolled quietly backwards down the dirt path through the open field.

57

SHE CALLED DWAYNE FIRST, and it felt like forever waiting for his truck to amble up the road.

When he finally arrived, he pulled off the paved road to the mouth of the path, easing his truck up beside Odie's car. She sat shivering in the driver's side, looking up into his window as he cranked the handle to roll it down.

"Jesus Christ, Odette. What happened to you?"

Odie kept her hands clenched on the steering wheel, her face as pale as her knuckles. She looked up at Dwayne, her chin dimpling as she struggled not to cry.

"I did something real bad, Dwayne. I'm fucked, and I'm scared."

Dwayne climbed out of his truck, his old jeans worn through at the knee and stained brown at the shins. He took off the thin flannel he was wearing over his white tank and handed it through Odie's window.

"Put that on and tell me about it."

58

WHEN DWAYNE and Odie passed through the mill's doorway, the scavengers that had been picking at Briggs and Alcott scattered. Rodents fled through cracks in the dilapidated building, armadillos and opossums snorting like pigs as they hightailed it into the noonday sun. Birds took to the rafters above that held the shoddy tin roof aloft, snakes wound their way into black crannies between outdated equipment long left behind.

Dwayne put his hand over his mouth and nose as he dared himself closer to the bodies, which had been thoroughly picked apart in just a few short hours, as if the creatures of Arkansas were eager to shit Briggs and Alcott out. Their meaty skeletons lay now in angel wings of viscera and the tattered remains of their clothing. The hole in the top of Alcott's skull overflowed with writhing maggots, their rice-shaped bodies stained crimson.

"Goddamn, Odie," Dwayne whispered, shaking his

head as he looked back at her. She stood leaning against the doorway wearing the long flannel, her shoulders hunched and her large brown eyes on the cement. "It looks like they've been here for days, not just a few hours."

"They were bad men, Dwayne," she said softly, shaking her head at the ground. "You know I'd never hurt someone that didn't deserve it. Briggs put my brother in the hospital and Alcott helped him lie about it."

"I can't even tell which is which." Dwayne had a strong stomach, but his face had gone a haunted gray, and he had to turn his back on the scene to keep his composure.

"What do I do?"

Odie looked on the verge of tears again. Dwayne came closer, carefully wrapping his arms around Odie, keeping his grip loose and cautious.

"Is this okay?"

When Odie nodded, he embraced her fully, letting her relax against his chest as she began to tremble.

"I'll take care of it. I might need some help, but I'll take care of it. The animals did a lot of work on the bodies for us. We'll put 'em in the cab of the truck and drive 'em up to Malvern. My stepdad has that junk yard out there. We'll crush 'em and leave 'em there. They won't ever be found, Odie."

He rubbed her back, his other hand moving to massage her neck gently.

"Does Dale know?"

Odie shook her head, pulling back from Dwayne and wiping the stubborn tears from her eyes.

"Then we should tell her. We're gonna need a third."

59

THE HEADLIGHTS BEAMED across the deserted highway, the lines on the road blurring past.

It all felt disorienting to Odie, who was in the passenger's side of Dwayne's truck with Dale behind the wheel. Ahead, they could see the brake lights on Briggs's pickup truck and the silhouette of Dwayne's halo of curly dark hair through the back window. The remains of the two police officers were in the back, wrapped tightly together in bungee cords and a bright blue tarp.

Dale was silent for the drive, only glancing at Odie when she thought she wasn't looking, but finally their eyes met. Odie spoke first.

"I'm so sorry," she said, trying to read the expression on Dale's face in the dim light.

"For what? Making me an accessory to murder?" Dale laughed grimly, eyes back on the road.

"For everything. My life, I guess. Lately it's just been one disaster after another, and I'm so scared I'm going to lose everyone I love. It's too much. This is too much for anyone to put up with."

"You're right, it's too much. Too much for one person, Odie. This isn't just drama, and it ain't your fault. You were raped. You had an abortion. Your little brother was shot. Life's never been easy for none of us, not a day in our lives. It's been shit, and it'll always be shit. All we've got is each other." Dale paused. "Light me a cigarette, will you?"

Odie opened the glove compartment and pulled out one of Dwayne's Zippos and a wrinkled soft carton of cigarettes. Dale leaned over as Odie put the cigarette between Dale's lips, flicking the lighter once, twice, three times until the cherry lit up bright orange. Dale pursed her lips and inhaled the smoke, then took the cigarette between her first two fingers and rested her wrist delicately back on the steering wheel.

"You know on Facebook, those posts that ask you to tag the friend you're most likely to go to jail with? Or how people say, 'Oh, I'd kill for my best friend' or 'I'd help her get away with murder'?" Dale glanced at Odie, a little smile curling her lips. "Well, I guess when I said it, I meant it. How many people could say the same?"

Odie parted her lips to speak, but nothing came. She remembered that kiss with Dale their first time at Club Trinity. It seemed so long ago, her heart aching. She wanted to kiss her now, felt her body drawn to Dale's like a magnet in the small cab of Dwayne's pickup. She reached over, her hand hovering over Dale's knee.

Dale sat up straight suddenly, her eyes on the road

with more intensity, her fingers gripping the steering wheel and nearly crushing the filter on the cigarette.

"What the fuck is Dwayne doing?"

Odie pulled her hand away just as suddenly, the moment broken. She could see the tailgate of Briggs's truck far ahead now, speeding away from them. Dwayne hit the horn over and over, then laid his hand on it as the truck flew.

"What the fuck is that?" Dale shouted, hitting the gas pedal. "Do you see that thing?"

Odie's head swerved left, then right, into the open plain of a darkened field. Dark except for a row of lights that seemed to be moving the same speed as the truck ahead of them.

"I don't know," Odie breathed out shakily. "A plane?"

"Fuck me if that's a plane," Dale said, pushing the old truck's gas to the mat. "It's a fucking UFO."

Odie barked out a laugh from sheer nervousness, her eyes still on the row of lights. Green, blue, and white, rotating so fast they blurred in a silvery gradient, smooth as water.

It all felt so absurd suddenly, and yet it was very real, right there before Odie's eyes, and Dale and Dwayne could see it too.

"Dwayne's trying to get ahead of it. Is it chasing us or him?"

Odie felt like she should be filming this, but no one could know they were out here, on this road, at this time, in these trucks. No one could ever know.

The lights fell back in line with Odie and Dale, as if

whatever was piloting the strange craft wanted to see inside the cab. It ran parallel to them, zipping closer so that Odie could see the strange balloon-like shape of the silvery exterior, a small black window at the helm. She thought for a moment she saw the gleam of an eye there, but it had to be the glass, or the lights, the confusion and panic that permeated this lonely highway. They were all utterly alone. And at the same time, very much not alone.

The radio clicked on, the dial moving up and down the stations wildly, the kaleidoscope of voices warping into static, a hellish, warbled song increasing in volume, a Satanic crescendo.

"I think it's looking at me," Odie whispered, the words catching in her throat. She felt as if she couldn't breathe.

The lights on the aircraft flickered out, the radio's warble dying and leaving a silence that twisted Odie's stomach in knots. Dale's foot hit the brake and Odie's shoulder slammed forward against the dashboard. The tires screeched and swerved on the asphalt to avoid hitting the tail end of Briggs's truck, which had come to a dead stop in the middle of the highway.

60

"YOU OKAY?"

Dale put the parking brake on and helped Odie right herself in her seat.

"Yeah."

Odie rotated her sore shoulder. It would be bruised tomorrow. She could already feel the knot rising.

They both looked up when they heard the creak of the truck door ahead of them opening. Dwayne stepped out and walked toward the front of the truck, where they could no longer see him.

"We need to check on Dwayne."

"Odie, I love you, and I care about Dwayne, but I ain't goin' out there. We don't know what the fuck's going on."

"I'm not leaving him. You stay here if you want to."

Odie's hands were trembling uncontrollably as she exited the truck. Her adrenaline made it difficult to feel her own feet as she began to walk toward Dwayne.

"Damn it!"

Dale climbed from the driver's side and joined Odie. Dale's hand sought hers, their fingers clasping tight as a clamshell.

They walked slowly, terrified of what they might see when they rounded the front of Briggs's truck. Dwayne was just standing there, his arms limp at his sides, staring straight ahead. Dale and Odie followed his gaze.

It was a doe, her hooves clopping softly on the pavement, her belly swollen with pregnancy. She turned her head to look at the three of them standing there looking at her, her large eyes blinking passively as the skin of her belly rippled and crawled with black veins, visible under the light spattering of fur in the bright headlights of the truck.

She fell over, braying, her feet kicking as a finger pushed through the thin, pulsating skin, then a fist, then a chubby arm. It was a human baby, peeling its way out of the doe, its bulbous head pushing through the hole its fist made as the deer's cries became gasping, strangled, unlike anything Odie had ever heard.

The baby burst out of the doe's stomach in a flood of organs and fluid, spilling endlessly across the highway and stretching toward them, curled like a talon. It was an impossible amount of blood. It reminded Odie of a popped dog tick.

Then the baby's own belly burst, flayed open by a beak. A robin climbed from the hole in the infant's stomach, shaking its feathers clean before taking flight, sleek and quick as a hawk.

Odie grasped Dwayne's arm and pulled him back, Dale holding Odie's arm and doing the same, the trio's stunned, stilted movements drawing them against the truck's face.

The doe was still alive, legs kicking, and the baby was laughing gutturally despite the large gape in its stomach. The deer clamored to her feet, hooves slipping in the viscera. The infant was still attached by an umbilical cord, strung to an organ hanging from the doe's stomach.

Twitching and braying, the doe ran off into the darkened plains, dragging the baby across the asphalt and dirt, into the black night.

61

THEY WERE SHAKEN, but there was still so much to be done under the cover of night. There was no time to regroup, no time to recover, only time to relive what they'd seen again and again in the silence of the long drive.

The terror of it seemed only to blend into the terror of all that had come before, when Odie and Dwayne had loaded the gnawed, dead bodies into the truck bed and a black snake had slithered out of Alcott's ribcage. When Dale had arrived to find the bodies already wrapped like mummies in the dusty blue tarp and vomited on Dwayne's front tire. The resignation that they all felt in their new reality.

They followed Dwayne's truck into the junk yard, tires rocking over the gravel. The place wasn't fenced in, didn't even have a sign marking it as a business. It couldn't be found on a map, and it didn't have a phone number in the yellow pages. It was truly local and truly isolated, and had probably hidden more bodies than the ones they were hauling in.

Dwayne turned off his headlights as they coasted slowly through the narrow paths formed by the hollowed vehicle shells, and he motioned through his window for Dale to do the same. It was a clear night, the moon and stars reflected in raw and twisted metal. Their eyes adjusted.

Dale stopped several yards behind Dwayne when he began rolling the truck onto the platform of the car crusher. It was more of a shredder, really, with jagged spinning gears that chewed metal as easily as a shark's teeth shredded flesh.

Dwayne hopped out of the truck and circled around to the levers that powered the industrial machine. It groaned awake, the teeth grinding and the engine puffing and purring loudly.

"Someone is going to hear this," Odie said. "Maybe it was a bad idea."

"It's the best option we've got. People hear weird shit out in the country all the time, no one goes to check on it."

"What if we get caught?"

"Hell, Odie. If we get caught, we'd just have to kill them too. Why not? We're in it now."

Dale watched the machine tip the truck, Dwayne's thin arms leaning hard into the lever with all his body weight. The metal began to scream as it was eaten, folding and breaking and caterwauling with every injury.

Odie put her hands over her ears and closed her eyes tightly, the sound muffled, blood swimming behind her eyes.

Bone and metal became mealy, spat out in a bucket like chewing tobacco.

PART 3
WHERE WILL YOU SPEND ETERNITY?

62

IT RAINED for seven days and seven nights.

63

THE THREE KEPT a low profile the week following the murders. They didn't see each other much in that time.

Odie poured herself into what her family now called Bub Duty: sitting at the hospital with Bubba Tucker, speaking to his comatose body as the machines beeped and breathed for him. Daddy was too drunk most of the time to reliably cover his shifts, so Odie took them on and welcomed the distraction.

Every now and then, she would turn on the news on the small box TV mounted on the wall and see Briggs and Alcott staring back at her. There was a statewide search for the missing policemen, one that had produced few leads so far.

64

Dale

I CAME by the hospital on the seventh day.

Odie was sleeping, curled up on one of them stiff reclining hospital chairs. She had a white sheet swaddled around her like a little baby, and her head had sunk into one of them hospital pillows filled with air.

The way she looked reminded me of when we were just little kids, sleeping over at each other's houses. She never wanted me to come over to her house, though. She always wanted to come to mine.

This was the first time I'd seen Bubba since he'd been shot. He was so pale, and his lips were chapped and white. His eyelids looked almost black, his cheeks swollen. When I touched his hand, it was as cold as the White River.

I'd known this boy since he was nine years old. He was just a little thing then, with big blue eyes and sandy hair. I remember every time spring rolled around, he'd go out looking for baby rabbits that'd been abandoned or lost by their mothers, and he'd try to raise 'em. It broke his little heart every time they died, but he just kept on doing it. He wanted so badly to save something good.

And that little boy I'd known had grown into this person, too old to be a child and too young to be a man. He'd got into some rough things here and there, the whole town knew it, but at his heart was something quietly compassionate, something the world tried so hard to whittle away.

I known him so long, it felt sometimes like he was my brother too. Now here he was, living by machines.

The more I thought about it, the more it pissed me the fuck off. Not just what happened with Bubba, which was senseless and cruel for no reason, but what had happened to Odie as well, and how little there was I could do about it.

And it got me thinkin' about how easy it was to get rid of them cops for Odie, how they got what was coming to them, and I don't feel one bit bad about it. One thing I reckoned, as I sat there watching Odie sleep, and watching Bubba dream the dreams of the almost-dead, was that the world would be a lot better place if Odette's rapist wasn't in it, like it was a better place now without them cops. And we'd gone far enough, what did one more dead bastard matter?

65

ODIE WOKE to Dale stroking the ridge of her nose lightly.

She swatted at Dale's hand, groaning, her hair a mess from being smashed into the weightless pillow. Dale laughed, sitting back down on the bedside commode and scooting it loudly next to Odie's recliner.

"I hate it when you do that," Odie said, sitting up and running her fingers through the tufts of her short hair.

"I tried shaking you, you just don't wake up that way. I don't know another soul on earth with a ticklish nose."

"What can I say, there aren't many folks like me."

"There aren't," Dale said. "That's why I love you."

It was quiet a moment, nothing but the sound of televisions in nearby hospital rooms chattering incoherently through the walls and the beep of Bubba's machines. Dale stood from her seat and shut the door to the room, and then it was very nearly silent.

"I been thinking," Dale said softly, returning to her seat on the commode, "about what we did."

"I don't want to talk about that, Dale. I just woke up."

"This is the best time and place to talk about it. No one can hear us."

"Well, then say what you're gonna say, because I don't want to talk about it no more after this."

"I been thinking about that boy who did that to you."

Odie said nothing, looking down at her hands, which lay palm-up in her lap, fingers curled limply. She studied the lines on her palms. The life line was short, but the love line went across the entire palm, a psychic at the Jackson County Fair once told her. She thought of it every time she looked at her hands since.

"What about him?"

"I did some research while you were sleeping. I found him on Facebook, his *real* name. It really is Will, and he'll be in Ohio over Christmas break, and I think we should go up there."

Odie stared at Dale, trying to wrap her mind around what she just heard. When she spoke next, there was a little tremble in her voice, like a fluttering wing.

"Are you crazy? Like, are you literally insane? Even if I wanted to, I don't know if I could even face him. It'd be like lookin' into the eyes of the Devil himself."

"Yeah, but you don't believe in the Devil, Odie, and he's just a boy. Just a little prick of a boy. He ain't even a cop. He's nobody."

Dale spat out the last sentence, her lip curling.

"You did what you did for Bubba. Why won't you do this for you?"

"Because I didn't do what I did. I mean, it wasn't really me, I don't think. I saw it all happen, but it was like I wasn't in my body at all, I wasn't in control."

"Because you wanted to do it, Odie. You wanted it bad. You can do it again, and me and Dwayne can help you this time. We'll look in the eye of the Devil for you if you can't do it yourself. Some folks don't deserve to live."

"Deserve? None of us deserves nothing. 'Deserve' was made up by people who already know they can get what they want."

Odie's eyes trailed to Bubba, to the white sheets pulled up to his chin, the dark bruises on his face from the trauma to his neck.

"Yeah, it was made up by people like Will. He thought he deserved to hurt you like that. So I'm proposin' we make up a new kind of 'deserve,' the kind where you get your pound of flesh."

"Shakespeare already done that."

"Fuck Shakespeare. That motherfucker's name was Will too. And anyway, we'll do it better. Arkansas-style."

66

Two Weeks Later

THEY STOPPED SOMEWHERE in northern Kentucky, rolling through a mostly empty town with all the hallmarks of a place left behind by technology, a place with abandoned factories hollowed out by time and the collapse of the short-lived titans of the industrial revolution. It was a town with a bank, a post office, a church, and a convenience store, one in which strangers were noticed, and it set Odie on edge.

It wasn't hard to recruit Dwayne. Once Dale and Odie told him about Will, it was like a red film had come down over his eyes. The three had caught a lust for blood fueled by a relentless anger that had been growing from a seed since the day they'd been born. They all wanted Will, wanted to tear him up like coyotes with a house cat. He wouldn't see it coming because people like Will never did.

Just outside of town, along the Kentucky and Ohio

border, they checked into an off-brand Motel 6. Dwayne paid in cash for two nights, a room with a king bed to share between the three. At the office desk, he printed his name on the register—a spiral notebook bent by the pressure of many ballpoint pens—as Jeffrey Lebowski.

The woman at the desk was a heavy smoker with dried too-dark makeup caked into the crevices around her lips. Her maroon lipstick crept jaggedly into the edges, giving her the appearance of a bleached-blonde straw-haired scarecrow. She didn't seem to get the Lebowski reference, just uttered something to Dwayne about *Jews* before handing over the keys to their room.

They'd been traveling for hours, their bodies cramped from stagnation, their stomachs rumbling and roiling for something warm to eat. Dwayne left in search of food and returned after an hour of scouring the surrounding and equally dead towns with a large pepperoni pizza and a case of Pabst Blue Ribbon at Odie's request. The three of them gathered on the bed, laying on their bellies to eat from the box.

"I've always wanted to go on a road trip," Dale said between greasy, dripping bites, her tongue sticking out to swirl the gooey mozzarella into her mouth. "I don't think I ever been out of Arkansas except for that trip up to Silver Dollar City a few years back with the church."

"I don't think a youth mission trip to Branson, Missouri counts."

"It does too count."

Dale went quiet a moment, opening her own can of beer and chugging it down in long swills.

"Not all of us got to go to college, Odie," she burped. "Not all of us got a free ride."

Tension bristled in the room, Dale's hackles raised and Odie's defenses coming down like an iron gate. They held each other's gazes until Odie's broke away.

"Ain't no such thing as a free ride. Everyone in this room ought to know that by now. I did everything I was told to do to find the kind of life people only dream of where we're from, and none of that was free. The scholarship don't matter. I was raped anyway. Bubba was shot anyway. Life is still *shit* anyway."

Odie's voice sounded like the warble of a broken needle on a record player, trembling and jumping in pitch as she fought back tears.

"I didn't mean it like that," Dale said, her blonde brow creasing over her cobalt blue eyes. Light colors streaked through them like ice daggers, whites yellowed by the motel light. "I just meant some of us don't have hope nor prayer. I'm not saying you didn't work hard, or that it's not all still shit. I'm just saying you had an opportunity and I didn't, Odie."

"We had the exact same opportunities, Dale. I just took mine, and you didn't."

Dwayne, who had been listening in silence with all the uncertainty of a man stuck in the middle of a problem he couldn't begin to solve, spoke softly now.

"If nothing matters, then why are we doing this?"

"Nothing matters, and that's *why* we're doing this."

Dale tipped her head back and finished her beer, and at the same time she reached for another and opened it.

Odie stood from the bed, her stomach twisted like a wrung-out rag. She went to the bathroom without a word, her heart pounding in her chest, in her ears, slamming the door and gripping the jaundiced plaster of the sink, leaning over the faucet and looking at her spit-stained reflection. Her palms were sweaty and slippery, her pupils dilating.

"Come on," she said quietly to Baby, willing it, whatever it was inside her, to come forth now, willing Baby to take away the electric shocks of anxiety that made her ribcage feel three times too big for her skin. "I can't breathe. Please."

Odie sank to the floor, setting her back against the bathtub, looking at the stray pubic hairs from guests past clinging to the corners of the caulked tile like little swirling smiles. She rubbed her temples, closing her eyes tightly.

No matter how she begged, Baby did not come. Baby was somewhere deep, traveling in Odie's mind, living a life in the subconscious part of her, she was certain.

She let out a soft cry, feeling suddenly abandoned, suddenly so alone.

But then a knock came at the door and Odie's tear-stained face squinted up at the doorknob as it turned, and there was Dwayne and Dale come like angels, haloed in the sickly light.

"You're alright, Odie," Dale said, crouching down next to her and putting her hand on her shoulder, squeezing, squeezing as if to say, *'You're here, and so are we.'*

"I'm sorry," Odie said, wrapping an arm around Dale

and another around Dwayne. He held up the beer in his hand, but it sloshed over the lip of the can anyway, a little splash landing in Odie's cropped hair. "I didn't mean to take it out on y'all. I'm sorry I said Missouri doesn't count."

Dale chuckled, petting the beer out of Odie's hair, running her fingers through until the locks were damp and fine again.

"It was a stupid argument anyway. Branson doesn't really count. It's basically Arkansas with Dolly Parton wannabes and log rides."

Dwayne untangled himself from their embrace. He reached into his back pocket and pulled out a plastic baggy of pungent weed, lifting it to his nose and inhaling deeply.

"Anyone up for a little oregano?"

67

THAT IS the moment Baby came springing forth like a grasshopper from the tall, tall grass of Odie's psyche, brown eyes growing large and glassy and desirous.

"Yes," Baby said. "I want."

68

THEY LAY on the bed on their backs, staring at the dimpled ceiling. Their eyes felt red and itchy, and the room was hazy with smoke.

Baby

BABY WANTED to know what it felt like to make love. Baby had made *fuck* before, but never love. And Baby knew from Odie what love was, because Odie loved Dwayne and Dale, but Dale most of all.

70

IT WAS Odie who kissed Dale first, a soft sweet kiss, cradling Dale's warm cheek in her palm. Dwayne rolled to his side to watch the two, propping his head up on his elbow.

"Nice," he said, lifting his thick brows.

"Shut up, Dwayne," Odie said softly, leaning over Dale's body to kiss him too, slow, languid, and sloppy.

Dale sat up on her elbows, joining the kiss now, their three tongues intermingling, tasting of pizza and beer and bitter.

71

THEIR BODIES WERE clumsy in their frolic, a blur of muscle and skin. Odie did not know where she began and they ended, knew only that she had longed for gentle and eager touch and now received it gladly.

There was something worshipful in Dwayne's kisses, something divine in Dale's moaning, a chorus of song in a dim motel room that climaxed with the rolling of their bodies into one.

Odie and Dale, spent and sated, curled into each other, and Dwayne stroked himself with both hands until he came into the open pizza box.

72

THE NEXT MORNING, the three stood in the bathroom at the large motel mirror, looking at each other's bare bodies.

Odie's breasts were heavy, the nipples large and purplish. Her arms were thick, shoulders broad, and she only had a slight curve at the waist. It was her hips that were wide, luxurious in their arch toward her thighs, and between them a thicket of dark pubic hair. The mess of her short hair made her look wild, the circles deep under her brown eyes.

Dale was thin and pale as paper, her chest small and nipples pink. Her body was covered in soft little white hairs that made her look as if she'd been painted with glitter, flat tummy drawing a straight line to her golden groin.

Dwayne stood between the two, tall and lanky and made of angles. His shoulders and elbows were sharp, his knees knobby. His hair was a mess of black curls, dark hair dripping down his white skin, covering his body. His thick cock hung like an elephant's trunk to his knee, and he was smiling at his companions in the mirror, and they were smiling back.

They couldn't be more different, the three of them, and yet there was a sameness about them, a oneness in the moment that made it clear what they must do.

Dwayne opened his shaving kit and made Odie sit on the toilet first. He stood over her while Dale sat on the edge of the tub and watched.

He clipped away the longest parts of her short hair, then doused her scalp in shaving cream, rolling his hands over her head and slapping it so the cream exploded against the walls, just to make her laugh. Dale took some of the shaving cream herself, fashioning a beard on her chin, then drawing a silly face on the length of Dwayne's penis.

Odie's head was shaved with a razor. She struggled to remain still as they giggled like naughty children. She watched the other two with a deep trust in her eyes, and they looked at her with the same.

Dwayne followed Odie, and then Dale, shorn locks falling like eyelashes brushed away from crying cheeks, and laughter filled the dark little motel room. They felt light as feathers, light as air, as if the loss of their hair was a baptism.

Then they showered together, rinsing away the stray hairs that covered their bodies, the fragrant shaving cream that clung to them like perfumed marshmallows, reborn.

73

THEY ARRIVED in the small Ohio town just as the winter sun kissed the tops of the pastel-colored houses of Hazel Grove, running parallel to each other in rows of greens, blues, yellows, and pinks. Nothing lay atop the perfectly manicured lawns, not a single lingering autumn leaf, no children's toys nor gardening tools. It wasn't until they pulled up to the curb of one of the houses—robin's egg blue with a blinding white roof—that Odie realized all the lawns were made of Astroturf.

Dwayne kept the engine running, a dull rattle shaking up the unshakable stillness of the neighborhood.

"We're too obvious here," Dale said.

She'd read Odie's mind.

"He said something about working downtown. We could circle around there, see if we see anything."

"And then what?"

Dwayne shifted the car back into drive, letting it crawl forward like a gator on its belly. He was still scanning, looking for any sign of Will at the end of the small cul-de-sac. A blonde girl rode a pink bike with silver streamers fluttering from the handles, round and round in circles in an empty driveway.

Dwayne lurched to a stop again and hung out the window, one hand resting atop the steering wheel.

"Hey! You know a guy named Will?"

The girl stopped her circling abruptly, her blue eyes widening. Still seated on her bike, she used her tiptoes to push herself back closer to the house, like a frightened rabbit creeping its way back to the brush.

Odie sighed and leaned over Dwayne so the little girl could see her face, see she came in peace.

"We're friends of his from college. We came to visit, but we don't know which house is his. Can you help us out?"

The little girl still looked stunned, like an arched-back possum in a floodlight. Then she lifted a finger and pointed at the yellow house diagonal from where they were parked.

Odie pulled back into the car. Dale pumped down the back passenger window as they rolled away.

"Thanks, kid!" Dale said, leaning up between the seats. "See, Dwayne? You just have to put on a little charm like Odie."

THEY PULLED the car between houses, out of the line of sight of any passersby. Dwayne handed Odie a pair of thick work gloves from under the seat. She moved to the trash bins stored at the side of the house.

She flipped open the recycling first and was met with a hot, stale soda can smell. She pulled at the crushed boxes inside the barrel, inspecting the labels. FedEx for Jenna, pizza for Will, We Heart Our Graduate sign with a photo of a pimple-faced ginger teenager, the name Justin in hand-lettered calligraphy underneath, pizza for Will, a soggy receipt, pizza for Will, employee discount for Will...

Odie got back into the car and slammed the door shut, pulling off the gloves. Her hands were already hot and covered in a salty film of sweat.

"I think he works at a place called Frank's Pizza Bar. That's gotta be it."

"Oh, that's what y'all was looking for, doing all

that?" Dale asked. "I could have told you where he works. It was on his Facebook profile."

Odie and Dwayne stared at Dale a beat, then burst out laughing.

"How the hell did you think I knew he lived in Hazel Grove? Y'all are dumbasses."

"See? This shit is why we shoulda had a plan," Dwayne said. "I thought we were all on the same page. You got too damn drunk last night, Dale."

Dwayne eased onto the street, cautious, but no cars were to be seen, an eerie quiet in Hazel Grove as if everyone had vanished in the rapture except the little girl on the bicycle going round and round.

75

THEY PARKED OUTSIDE AND WAITED, not really knowing if he'd be on shift or not.

It was night before they saw him, greasy-faced and smoking a cigarette in the alley beside Frank's Pizza Bar. Odie had forgotten how very young he looked, then remembered he was younger than her, and only a year older than Bubba. His face was boyish as ever, scraggly blonde hairs waving from his chin, full red cheeks, a cross between a toddler and a billy goat.

It was the first time she was looking at him sober, without the haze of a bad night over her vision, the shock of what he had done to her, the questions about whether it was something she had deserved.

He seemed smaller, too, or perhaps it was that Odie felt bigger now in so many ways.

"That him?" Dwayne asked, an unlit cigarette between his lips so that he talked with a growl.

"Yeah, that's him."

"Looks like a damn goat."

"That's what I was just thinking," Dale said, no sense of mirth in her voice. She pressed her face to the window. "What now?"

"I reckon we wait for him to get off work. Could be a while, it's a bar after all."

"What if we went in?"

Dwayne and Odie looked back at Dale, twin looks of disbelief on their faces.

"You crazy? That's a surefire way to get caught."

"Well, hear me out. What's more suspicious, going to the bar and having a few drinks or sitting out in the car, scoping the place, plain as day to every surveillance camera on the damn block?"

As they crossed the street, Odie kept her eyes focused on the bar's door, anywhere but on Will, who was smoking his cigarette down to the filter.

It was a difficult thing to do, to keep focused with a fire growing in her belly, rage and hunger eating at the lining of her stomach like alligator gar, death by a thousand gnawing teeth.

There was a skinny guy in a polo leaning against the wall, half-blocking the door, one earbud in as he scrolled his iPod. When the three moved to breeze past him, he stuck his leg out.

"Whoa, there's a cover charge. We have a band playing tonight."

"How much?"

Odie was the first to pull out her wallet, knowing damn well she probably didn't have the money, but also knowing they couldn't afford to have a confrontation on the street. Then a voice froze her hands on the cracked pleather.

76

"CHILL, LAYTON."

Will's voice from behind the three, that scratchy, almost pubescent sound coming from the pink lips of a jock asshole.

Odie turned around, eyes meeting his for the first time since that morning he dropped her off in Harvard Square.

She could feel the white melting into the color of her face like spreading frost, the breath knocked from her gut, leaving her lips feeling blue. But she could tell from his eyes he did not recognize her, or if he did, it was only vaguely.

"There's no cover charge, he's just fucking with you."

"Thanks for blowing it, Will."

The one called Layton had the collar of his polo popped so it tickled his earlobes. One lobe was pierced with a large, square-cut cubic zirconia.

"You're lucky he did," Dwayne said, stepping up next to Layton.

Dwayne looked small next to him, wiry, but he was swamp-rat tough and Layton was a preppy, soft suburbanite.

"If you'd taken us for a ride, I'd've beat your ass right here on the street. There's a curb right over there calling your name."

"Fellas, fellas," Will said placatingly. "There's no need to harsh the mellow. We're all gentlemen here."

He glanced at Odie and Dale. He seemed to find them strange, almost alien-like creatures with their shaved heads, their eerie similarity and uniform black T-shirts.

"And ladies, of course. Please, please, go in and make yourselves at home. Our casa es su casa at Frank's."

Dale smirked and shouldered past Layton. If Dale or Dwayne had feelings one way or another about Will in that moment, they did not reveal them. Instead, Dwayne just gave Will a nod, as if in solidarity, the Bro Code upheld and all was right with the world.

The inside of Frank's Pizza Bar was smokey, scent of nicotine fused with oven-baked pizza and the sour smell of beer. There was music on the little step-up they called a stage, but it wasn't a band, just a camouflage-jacketed veteran with an American flag do-rag sucked to his bald white head singing "Gangster's Paradise" on the karaoke machine.

No one seemed to notice or care that they were there, odd as they looked among the locals. Odie knew

Will worked at a pizza place, but she had pictured something a little classier given the obvious wealth of his parents. He was getting the finest education at one of the most prestigious universities in the world. His dad was a hospital administrator, his mom a civil lawyer, according to Facebook. He must have chosen to work here for the free pizza and booze, for the fact that no one in his family would be caught dead here, if for nothing else.

This was the moment Odie realized she was giving Will too much thought. She was here to do a job, and the job was to wipe the shit stain that was Will from the face of the earth.

77

THEY EACH HAD three cans of PBR. They set them up like bowling pins on the bar once they'd emptied them and rolled tightly balled wet napkins down the makeshift lane. They kept score on a napkin, and a few of the other patrons, a rough, dead-eyed crowd bored of the music, joined in, their laughter slurred, hanging onto each other's shoulders like apes.

Every now and then Odie caught a glimpse of Will in the back, shoving pizzas into the oven or taking them out, his white T-shirt stained red and orange and yellow with pizza sauce old and new. He wiped his sweaty upper lip with the back of his sweaty arm.

When she closed her eyes, she could smell him. Salty. Hear him. The rough panting of his sour breath against her neck, the nip of his teeth grazing her skin, her ear. His hands on her wrists, his legs splayed atop hers, bare feet holding her ankles apart.

Odie's expression twisted into one of disgust as she lost herself for a moment in the memory, pulse rising with the searing heat in her face. Tears mingled with the sweat in her eyelashes, the noise around her coming to a warbling halt.

Then Odie was back in the bar, Dale with her arm thrown around her, shaking her gently.

"You're okay, Odie. You're okay."

THEY LEFT the bar at closing time like any other patron, moving sluggish and tired out the door to blend in with the haggard regulars. The three stumbled, holding each other up, their laughter filling the void of an otherwise dead street.

When they reached the car, Dwayne started it up and let it sit idling, the heat from the exhaust pipe puffing plumes of smoke in the cold air like a simmering dragon.

"What now?" Dale asked, her wrists resting on the shoulders of Dwayne's and Odie's seats, her blue eyes dark in the dim car.

"I don't know. We wait? See if he's the last one left inside. If he stays, we'll go in. If he leaves, we'll follow."

"We ought to have planned this better."

"Nah," Dale said. "Plans are bad luck. We haven't made a plan yet. Why start now?"

"Kill the cop inside your mind," Baby whispered from Odie's lips, and they all nodded in agreement.

Baby always knew just what to say, but chaos was more than a catch phrase. It was a calling.

79

LIFE WAS CHAOS.

Utterly unpredictable.

Less than two months ago, Odie thought she was going to finish college, graduate with honors, stay in the city, get a decent job somewhere and have a mundane life. Sure, she needed to kick her alcohol habit sometime on the way, but the point is that it was all possible. Possible in a way it had never been before. That was all gone now.

The dream had been hollowed out, and the shell of it had been filled with rage. Rage and Baby.

Maybe the only way to get through this was by the skin of their teeth.

80

THEY WATCHED as the bartender left out the front door and locked it, but Will had not come out yet.

"Did that Layton guy leave yet?"

Dale pulled a taser from under the driver's seat. They were hunting now.

Odie could feel her pupils blown wide as a mountain lion's.

"I don't know, but I wouldn't mind wringing his neck, neither," Dwayne said. "Odette, get the gun out the glove box."

Odie did as Dwayne said while he turned the car's ignition off, the rumbling exhaust cutting out and leaving the dead street cast in a silence that could only be described as loud. Dwayne went around the back of the car and pulled out a metal baseball bat, swinging it once, then putting it over his shoulder before pulling a cigarette with his teeth from a soft pack in his hand.

Dale and Odie climbed out of the car, Dale rubbing at her prickly bald head, dancing on her toes. Ready.

The three stood there for a moment on the quiet street, staring at Frank's Pizza Bar in a sort of meditative tranquility, as if they were standing in the hollow tail of a tornado and the rest of the world spun on around them, indifferent to their plans.

"Are we sure about this?" Odie asked, putting Dwayne's pearl-handled revolver down the front of her pants. "Y'all ain't killed no one yet. You still have a way out of this."

"But we don't want out, Odie," Dale said. "This ain't just for you."

81

IT SMELLED of rot and yeast, stray pizza toppings littering the alleyway and a pile of black trash bags leaning precariously against an over-full dumpster. They went in through the back door.

The rumbling of the industrial refrigerators masked the sound of their footsteps. Dwayne was leading, the baseball bat balanced on his shoulder, his fist gripping it until his knuckles turned translucent white. There was a sink running, the clatter and clash of metal pizza trays as they were thrown atop a rack to dry.

The three peered around the corner of the fridge shielding them from view. Will was washing dishes and doing a half-assed job of it.

Dwayne nudged Odie forward.

Her hand gripped the handle of the gun in the front of her pants, but it was all the movement she made as she watched the boy who had raped her do the innocuous task of closing up shop for the night. This boy, who was allowed to carry on with his little life in the suburbs, living in his parents' pastel house during holiday breaks and returning to their prestigious school to be pet and fawned over by professors. None of them knew who he was, not really.

Dwayne gently nudged Odie again, and when she made no movement again, it was Dale who stepped out.

"Hey!" Dale barked, leaning against the refrigerator.

Will jerked in surprise, then whipped around, dropping the tray he'd been washing. Suds sloshed over the countertop and leaked onto the already wet terracotta floor.

"Jesus Christ!"

"Not even close," Dale said with a little smile. Will was tall, but she was looking down on him all the same.

"Did you leave something in the bar?"

"Nope."

An uneasy silence hung between them, Dale's icy blue eyes never leaving Will's. Dwayne stepped out from behind the refrigerator with his baseball bat, and after a few deep breaths, Odie followed, the pearl-handle of the revolver visibly peeking over her waistband.

Will was taking it all in, wiping his hands on his apron. His eyes studied them, their identical bald heads and black T-shirts. Despite their different features, there was an odd sense that they were the same creature, a Cerberus standing before him, a three-headed thing with teeth.

"If you want to rob the place, you can take what you want. I don't give a shit about any of this," Will said with a vague wave around the kitchen. "Seriously, I'll open the register for you. The fuck do I care?"

"We ain't here for money. We never had money before, we don't need it now."

Dwayne let the baseball bat drop idly in an arc, swinging it back up to his shoulder.

"You really don't remember me at all, do you?" Odie asked quietly, pulling the gun from her waistband. "You don't remember what you did to me? It was less than two months ago."

Will's hands went up the moment the gun was pulled free, even though she hadn't yet pointed it at him. He studied Odie's face long and hard for the first time, his blue eyes pinched into a squint, brows furrowed hard. It was barely noticeable, but he was quivering now, his heart beating so hard Odie could almost see it pulsing through his apron.

"I don't know you. I've never seen you before in my life."

Odie barked a laugh suddenly, a violent sound.

"Never seen me before. Well, you *were* drunk. Not that that's any excuse. You had enough of your faculties about you that you hid the condom when we got back to your place. Enough of your faculties to hold me down and rape me."

"Whoa, rape? Stop right there, because you don't know what the fuck you're talking abou—"

Dwayne dropped the bat again, swinging it up with a *whoosh*. It struck Will under the chin, his head snapping up and back hard. Teeth spat in a bloody arc, clattering against the wall and floor like rain on a tin roof.

82

THEY STOOD OVER WILL, their three heads looking down at him in the dampened fluorescent light.

It was Dwayne who grabbed Will by his thinning hair, handing off the baseball bat to Dale before dragging him toward the staff bathroom. It was an ill-lit closet with a mildewed mop bucket inside, the base of the toilet stained brown, appearing darker than it really was in the dim light.

Will was holding his mouth as blood leaked from between his fingers like a sieve, his other hand helping support himself on his knees as he was mercilessly led.

"Put the gun on him, Odie," Dwayne said, hauling Will's weight into the small space. His head was hanging over the toilet. He spat blood into the bowl. When he spoke, his voice was thick from swelling.

"What do you want?" Will was weeping, putting a hand up to block his face, even though no blow was coming. "I don't know you people. Just tell me what you want, I'll give it to you. I'll call my parents, they'll do anything you want."

"I think your parents had a hand in this mess," Dale said, her cheek resting against the door frame. "Maybe just a little bit. They did raise an entitled little fuck boy. What could we possibly want from them that they haven't already given us? You're a pussy served up on a platter."

Odie handed the gun to Dale, who leveled it at Will's head. Her stomach cramped, her hands moving to her lower belly as she groaned softly.

"You put something inside me when you raped me, Will. Something more than your pathetic little cock. I tried to get rid of it, but it stuck around. And now it's going to be the reason you die."

83

ODIE DROPPED to her knees beside Will, panting softly now as she spoke, the anger climbing up her throat and causing her voice to quake. It was pure, unadulterated rage, building since the moment he'd held her down, and everything that had happened since that moment had only been gasoline.

Baby

BABY SLAMMED the toilet seat down on Will's head, a gleeful laugh crawling up its throat. The toilet seat came down on Will again and again, an infant with a rattle.

WILL'S hand lashed out at Odie, his body thrashing to try to free himself from the violence of the beating like a fox in a snare. Odie pushed the back of his neck deeper into the bowl, his bloodied mouth screaming, bubbling the toilet water pink.

Baby

BABY SAT atop the thrashing seat, bouncing and giggling madly. Each time he thrashed, Baby brought their weight down on his neck, again and again and again, with glee.

87

WHEN WILL WENT STILL, Odie released him, his body slumping away from the toilet and against the wall, leaving a crimson smear. His eyes were open, bulging, the veins blown and whites filled with blood. His lips were blue and he gasped up at the three like a fish, a disk in his neck visible through the skin.

Baby

"YOU CAN'T MOVE?" Baby asked, pouting and clicking its tongue. "That's too bad."

89

DALE TOOK one leg and Dwayne took the other, dragging Will's dead weight back into the kitchen. He lay flat on his back, his eyes wide open and swimming, his jaw shattered and neck black with bruises. Odie, Dale, and Dwayne panted at each other like dogs.

90

THEN THEIR BOOTS came down like anvils, and the force of their rage did not let up. Not until Will's head was a pulped melon, the pulverized pieces spilling across the tile in a wide halo.

91

THEY LEFT the slaughter there in the kitchen. They didn't bother to clean or conceal anything. If they were caught, they simply did not care.

92

LET IT BE A WARNING.

PART 4

BEFORE I FORMED YOU IN THE WOMB, I KNEW YOU

93

IT WAS cold back in Kentucky.

Dwayne pulled his truck off the highway and onto a dirt road, far enough into the trees that when they covered the hood with a forest green tarp it was no longer visible from the road. They each shouldered their backpacks, small tents, and sleeping bags, then trekked further into the trees until they were certain a small fire wouldn't draw any notice from the road.

A light dusting of snow was falling, the temperatures plummeting as each minute of day passed into night. Dwayne gathered the firewood while Odie and Dale set up their tents as close to the makeshift fire pit as possible. They had each been quiet since they'd left Ohio, only speaking when absolutely necessary, lost in thought and memory of the night before.

"The wood's getting wet," Dwayne muttered, tossing another small tarp over what he had gathered so far. "It's going to be a rough night. I'm not even sure I can get a fire going with all this damp."

"We're gonna have to or we'll freeze to death," said Dale, tromping over the wet leaves and using gloved hands to uncover the dry stuff beneath. "We'll make it work. The hard part is getting it started. We can take turns keeping it going throughout the night."

"No, you two get some sleep. I don't mind staying up."

Dwayne pulled a Zippo out of his worn camouflage cargo pants, flicking it open and lighting one of the dried leaves. He tossed it on top of the small pit and began to stoke it with a thin stick, pushing the growing flame around the pit. He worked the fire like this for fifteen minutes, coaxing the flame to a lapping tongue. Despite the cold, he wiped sweat from his beading brow with the back of his hand until the fire was about the height of his knee.

He sat back on the hard ground, watching the fire in silence while Odie and Dale finished constructing their tents. When they came to the fire, they were wrapped in their sleeping bags. Odie put Dwayne's over his shoulders and wrapped him up tightly before taking a seat herself.

"There are no two people in the world I'd rather be with right now," he said, looking up at Odie, then Dale, before pulling a rolled joint out of the breast pocket of his shirt and lighting it.

The skunk smell of his homegrown weed permeated the small encampment, his lips pursing as he sucked and held the smoke with his chest puffed out, then exhaled quietly with the skill of a practiced stoner.

"I'd always wondered what I was supposed to be doing on this earth. Now I know it's this."

"Camping in the woods with fags?" Dale reached for the joint and Dwayne handed it over gladly.

"Killing rapists," he said, leaning back on his elbows. "For Odette."

Odie kept her eyes on the fire, resting her cheek in her hand, half-hiding her soft smile.

"For Odette," Dale agreed with a nod before tilting her head back and shaping her mouth into an O, blowing smoke rings against the stars, watching them expand and disappear into darkness.

94

ODIE WOKE in her tent in a fever, sweat prickling her skin like phantom spider legs. She sat up, wiping at her face with her palms; they were freezing cold despite the burning heat deep in the flesh.

Dale crawled out of her tent and crept over to Odie's. As she passed Dwayne, whose eyes were heavy as he kept watch over the fire, he lifted his hand and gave her a little thumbs up and encouraging smile before going back to staring at the flames.

Dale nodded and unzipped Odie's tent, whispering softly, "Odie?"

Odie didn't stir, her body rising and falling with her quiet snores. Dale crouched outside the tent, reached for Odie's thickly socked foot and squeezed her toes lightly.

"Mm?" Odie groaned softly, shifting in her sleeping bag.

"Is it okay if I come in? It's cold in my tent."

Dale's voice shook with the power of her trembling,

even though her own sleeping bag was wrapped around her shoulders.

It took Odie a few moments to register what Dale had said, and at first Dale was certain Odie had fallen back to sleep. But then she pried the zipper of her sleeping bag open, inviting Dale to cuddle against her body.

Dale smiled, eager, and moved into the tent, zipping it up behind her and settling down in the confines of the small nylon dome. Odie let her arm fall limply over Dale's side, her hand touching the warm skin of her lower back.

"Hey," Dale said in greeting, smiling in the dark.

"Hey," Odie replied, smiling back with her eyes still closed.

"2010 has been kind of crazy, huh?"

Odie laughed. All the tension of the previous weeks had left her body, it seemed. She felt like she felt last summer, the summer before she had left for college, the summer when the world had felt full of possibility. She was going to be the first in her family to get a college degree, and she had been promised that a college degree meant stability, hope for a brighter future than the past she had come from, and an end to the relentless ennui of poverty and hopelessness. To have discovered it was all a lie, that none of it mattered, had made her feel insane.

"I think that's an understatement."

Dale giggled, covering her mouth. Even in the dark, she was self-conscious of her smile.

"Maybe, but as batshit insane as it's been, I'm so glad I've gotten to spend this time with you."

Odie was silent, so silent that Dale feared she had said something wrong, or that Odie had fallen back to sleep.

"I'm glad too," she said softly, moving her hand from the small of Dale's back, up to touch her cold cheek in the darkness. Her thumb found her lips, tracing the shape of the bottom one, then the top, playing at the Cupid's bow.

"This okay?"

"Yes, it's okay," Dale said. "Very okay."

"I don't feel like the same person I was before."

"That's because you're stronger, Odie. You're the strongest, most loyal person I've ever known."

"I couldn't have done any of this without you and Dwayne," Odie whispered. "Even if it all goes to shit, it'd have been worth it."

She leaned in, pressing her forehead to Dale's and letting the blood in their veins flush their cold skin with warmth.

"Can I kiss you?"

They whispered in unison, their noses touching as they laughed, their breath intermingling between their lips as Odie pushed her hips forward. She squeezed Dale's middle against her, Dale's body eager to be close, their lips playing at each other's until they met in a deep kiss.

Odie parted her lips, letting Dale inside, and Dale pressed her tongue to the tip of Odie's.

"I've wanted this," Odie said breathlessly against

Dale's lips. She sucked on her tongue and opened her mouth wider to massage the corners of her mouth.

"I thought you'd never admit it," Dale said when they parted, looking at each other in the dim light, eyes adjusting, eyes seeing only as far as each other in the dark of the tent.

Odie took the hem of Dale's shirt and pulled it over her head, then allowed Dale to do the same to her, their hair mussed and wild from the static of their sweaters.

When they touched each other's breasts, static pricked their skin with a little shock, which made them giggle, each in turn shushing the other.

"Dwayne knows, he's cool with it," Dale said as she sucked dark-spotted kisses against Odie's neck, her hands pushing her pants down her thighs. Dale slipped her palm into Odie's panties, her fingers curling to open her lips, parting the hair like the Red Sea.

"It's so hot that you don't shave," Dale said, her head ducking to trace Odie's collar bone. "Are you sure this is okay?"

"God, yes," Odie said, bucking her hips against the curl of Dale's fingers.

Neither Dale nor Odie felt cold anymore.

Dale embraced Odie with her free arm, lifting her into a sitting position. Dale draped her left leg over Odie's right thigh, and Odie's left leg over her own right thigh. They held each other close, Dale's hand slipping up to cradle the back of Odie's head, fingers curling into her short, dark hair as she tilted her chin up and kissed her throat.

Her fingers between Odie's pussy lips worked at the

swollen nub of her clitoris, dipping into her vagina to lubricate her with the wet discharge.

She pulled her hand away just as Odie began to gasp, edging her, both hands now gripping her ass to pull their groins together.

It took some awkward maneuvering, each of them unable to contain the giggles between their huffs of pleasure, before they were able to rub their clits together, the tender flesh slicking like pomegranate seeds.

Heat clung to the inside of the tent, rolling down the vinyl and smelling of salt and damp. Odie rocked her hips forward, letting gravity do the work of pushing Dale back beneath her. Her shaved head was cradled by the built-in pillow of the sleeping bag, her eyes wide and dark.

"What?" Odie panted against Dale's parted lips, their breath biting from the cheap beer.

"Nothing. I just never seen you like this."

"Like what?"

Odie began to draw back, but Dale's rough palm held the back of her neck with a soft pressure.

"Like you know what you want. I like it. I like it a whole lot."

Odie sank her hips between her legs, the warmth of her against her belly like a sun-drenched blanket of moss.

Nothing about Dale had changed. It was *Odie* who had changed.

"I want you. I've always wanted you."

"I know. I just never thought you'd say it."

Dale's hand slipped from the back of Odie's neck to the bristles of her dark hair, and she kissed her again and again.

Odie

I WAS LAYING on my back with Dale's sleeping face pressed to my armpit when I felt the pain, sharp in my belly like a fingernail trying to whittle its way through. I sat up and clamped a hand over my mouth, the other fumbling with the zipper on the tent until I was pushing free of the door and spilling out into the cold night air.

The fire was nothing but ash and ember now, steam rising into the low canopies of the trees. My stumbling dragged rivulets into the dark soil, leaving dripping coagulated blood seeds planted in my wake.

I was hurrying from the campsite so as not to wake Dwayne or Dale, but when I passed Dwayne's tent, I saw that it was open and empty.

"Dwayne?" I hissed as I pushed through grown-up brambles, tangles of kudzu vines twisted like snakes with the poison ivy that crept along the forest floor.

It was only now I realized I was still naked, felt the

sting of air on the bites Dale left on my breasts. There was a meager attempt to cover myself as thorns bit at my calves, one arm at my chest, the other hand slipping between my legs to feel the hot blood tangled in my pubic hair.

I collapsed onto my knees at the lip of a puddle, the reflection of the moon cutting through the leaves above like lasers. My stomach felt bloated and hard above my groin. I fell back on my ass, the puddle licking at my skin as I balanced my hands behind me, my heels pressed into the muddy water, sliding in the slick as my legs dropped open.

I cried out now, a scream so agonized I didn't recognize it as my own until the spit caught in my throat, and I choked. My head fell back between my shoulder blades. I watched the shadows of the trees flicker like mirages, a phantom light flooding the darkness from a source I could not see.

Again the pain came like a rapid knock at a door, sharp and tearing and thumping wildly as my pulse. My fingers dug into the earth to the knuckles. I twisted my neck and screamed again. My vagina was opening like a mouth and something was coming through.

Odie

I REACHED between my legs and felt the hard, jagged edge of something foreign, slick with a film of fluid. Whatever it was came through like a crooked elbow with no hand. I looked down at the limb waving wildly from my vagina, curling and thumping against my belly. It was a crawdad tail.

Odie

I THOUGHT of the night my cousin had her firstborn. We were both thirteen. She carried the baby in her stomach like a toddler carrying a bowling ball. I waited in the hallway of the small-town hospital, the very hospital I had been born, and my father, and his father. A terrible screaming broke through the sterile buzz and beep of machines in a hospital that had otherwise been unchanged for a century. My cousin's epidural hadn't worked, and her adolescent body was giving birth full-feeling, her cries like a volley of arrows.

Odie

I FOUND MY VOICE, but it was bleating and weak, crying out now for Dale, for Dwayne, for anyone who could hear me. Then I realized, if they could hear me, they might have come by now.

Tears dripped from my jaw, joining the sweat slithering between my breasts and gathering in my navel. I straightened my back and pushed, my teeth snapping shut into a growling grimace, the skin between my brows drawn hard into peaks.

Odie

WHEN WHAT WAS inside me finally came spilling into the puddle, I felt numb with relief. I panted hard, my lips quivering, face drained of blood as I clamored to sit up, to see it. The gray thing was thrashing in the water, tugging on the umbilical cord still tethered inside me.

I grasped at it like a trout fighting a fishing line, slipping through my fingers until I was finally able to pin it down in a hold. I lifted it from the puddle, the strobing lights in the trees behind me glittering across its dolphin-like skin. Its body was curled like a crawdad's, two large black eyes sitting round as saucers with an entire galaxy inside, no lids save for a thin blinking membrane. Its single stump of an arm reached, padding my cheek, a small round mouth gawping with a single egg tooth.

I wept because it was beautiful. I wept because it

was Baby, my baby that I had made, and I knew now that I had been carrying it long before I was raped.

Every strange or terrifying thing that had ever happened to me or that I had ever felt, through all of it, there had been this thing inside me, carrying me too. I drew it close to my chest and lay back against the earth, heaving with a sudden sob as I kissed its slick head and it continued to pat pat pat at me as if to comfort me. Then I watched as the gleaming beads of its eyes rolled like glass spheres to look up at the lights that had now enveloped us both.

I saw what it saw, the spinning lights of the flying saucer eclipsing the moon, but this time I was not afraid. Baby began to lift from my arms, its little crawdad tail curling, it's bulb-like eyes glittering with the worlds that lived inside me.

"Goodbye," Baby chirped, waving its smooth limbs, its rough tail. "Goodbye, and thank you!"

100

Odie

THE UMBILICAL CORD pulled from inside me, the placenta it was attached to ballooning out from my vagina and dragging into the puddle. I lurched forward as quickly as I could, grasping at it as it slipped through my fingers. I bit into it, tearing the chewy cord with my teeth, thrashing my head as the taste of blood and dirt filled my mouth. I severed it.

I watched the baby-thing rise higher into the trees, that little limb waving and its warbling voice fading with distance. The lights strobed in the spaces between the leaves, turning the surrounding woods into a disco. I lifted a bloodied hand and waved back, my mouth smeared with the pinkish fluid that spilled from the umbilical cord.

There was an eruption of light like the flash of a camera big as a satellite, my forearm held aloft to save my burning retinas. The light was hot, even from this distance, and I felt the hair on my arms and legs curl. And then it, and the baby-thing, were gone.

I don't know when I remembered to breathe, but the breath came in a loud animal-whimper, the placenta between my legs blooming from my vagina at last and spilling between my thighs. I reached for it, then collapsed onto my back, the slick thing laying between my breasts with the umbilical cord snaking down the line of my navel.

The leaves fluttered. Dale was running toward me. Her calloused hands grasped at my arms to lift me into a seated position, the placenta spilling into the cradle of my arms like a slippery child.

"Odie?"

Dale's hands stroked the slimy fluid away from my mouth. My skin was reddened with something like a sunburn, tender and hot.

Dale's voice sounded far away, the allure of sleep, of that blanket of blessed exhaustion, settling over me and my flaking skin. Her arm looped around my back, the other bracing beneath the crooks of my knees. She lifted me as my head drooped back.

"I think it's done now," I said. "It's gone."

Back at the camp site, Dwayne was gone too.

101

Dwayne

I WAS TAKING a piss when it happened.

The lights were moving through the trees, and I almost immediately knew what they were. It wasn't too long ago those very same lights chased us down the highway. I wondered if they been following us all along.

I had my pants around my ankles, and I couldn't just stop mid-stream, even when my body felt suddenly weightless and the leaves around me began to shift. I'm not ashamed to admit I pissed on myself a little. The ancient tree trunks rattled, like they was gonna come right up out the earth.

I called for Dale and Odie, but the words sounded nothing like words at all, just a tone reverberating within the beam of light that hit me hot as an iron.

I flailed my arms wildly when my feet left the ground, my body rotating so that I was on my back, looking up into the bright light of Heaven itself.

It looked like the muscles I used to dig up around the pond at my daddy's house before he passed. It opened up its big mouth and something like a tongue came flopping out, licking at my body. It was like being touched by God.

The thin skin on my nose and dick began to blister and burn, peeling away like old paint, but I didn't feel no pain at all. It felt euphoric, a deep burning in my belly and a crawling notion in my thighs that made me hard as a rock.

The tree limbs seemed to part for me as I was carried by the beam of light, up and up until I was bowled over on that licking tongue. My clothes had all burned away, my skin raw and pink. My chapped lips parted in a wide O, my eyes filled with the ecstasy of a celestial union.

I felt myself cum at last over the tongue that licked me into the warm hole of Heaven's gate, and I live there now among the curious angels.

Christmas Day
Odie

I DROPPED the placenta into the bubbling jam of fruit and sugar. I mashed it down, watching the pinkish fluid inside erupt and fill the hollow of the wooden mixing spoon before mingling with the bloody swill of cherries.

This organ we'd made, Baby and me, sank into the filling and burst like a hot plum, the membranous skins of cherry and placenta indistinguishable now from one another.

Denise turned from where she'd been rubbing brown sugar over the ham Daddy had won in a work raffle at the factory, which would caramelize into a sweet crust in the oven.

"It's a little thin, Baby Girl. Add another half-cup of sugar."

She turned back to open a can of pineapple, the aluminum scraping against the cracked countertop, yellowed in the dim kitchen light. Daddy passed through the kitchen, grabbing two beers from the fridge in one large paw. He looked at the ham, then leaned to look over my shoulder as I shook the sugar into the mix, a white spiral dissolving into the deep crimson color.

"Looks good. Smells good, too, Odette," he said, hot vodka breath on my shoulder.

"Back up. You stink."

I nudged him back with my elbow, shifting on my feet as I stirred and stirred.

"Well, hell. You don't want to be here with your family on Christmas? You too good for us now you're all educated and worldly?"

"I was just joking," I said, turning my chin over my shoulder and giving him a smile. "I love you, Daddy."

This seemed to take him by surprise. He shifted the beers into his other paw, blinking his light eyes. His swollen face deflated as the puff of anger left it.

"I love you too, Sweetheart. Damn. Thought you was serious."

"Nah," I said, stirring the pot. "I'm happy to be here. Happy Bub's home. Happy we're all together."

He seemed appeased by that. I heard his footsteps behind me, passing into the living room where *A Christmas Story* was playing on a loop. A beer can hissed. I listened to his pacing as he idly watched and swigged.

I wove the top of the pie into a lattice and popped it in the oven.

Odie

THERE WAS no table to gather around.

Me and Denise fixed our plates of ham, mashed potatoes, cornbread dressing, baked beans, and rolls and found a place in the living room to sit. Daddy was in his recliner. Denise sat on the sofa.

I fixed a plate for Bubba, who sat in a corner in a wheelchair. The drugs made him unsteady on his feet. His plate only had a heap of mashed potatoes and gravy, but luckily that was his favorite. I was glad about that. I gave him a lot because his time in the hospital had made him thin. His healing throat could only do liquids and soft solids. His neck and chin was still bruised, the purple veins beneath the green skin like spider silk.

I sat in the floor between the recliner and the wheelchair so I could be close to Bub, my legs criss-cross-apple-sauced as I pulled apart my roll and dipped it in giblet gravy. Daddy didn't make himself a plate, instead pacing between the kitchen to pick at the ham and take bites of baked bean from the glass dish, his bedroom to wash it down with vodka, and the living room where he returned to his beer and laughed candidly at *A Christmas Story* from his recliner.

"I'm sure glad you're home, Bub," I said as I chewed my roll, the butter and gravy washing over my tongue.

"I'm sure glad, too."

When he spoke his mouth barely opened, his jaw still healing from the trauma to his neck, a red crescent moon of burst blood vessels cradling the iris of his left eye. He took small bites of the soft potatoes.

Denise was slumped back in the crook of the sofa with her plate in her lap, her kohl-lined eyes heavy-lidded. It was early afternoon, but it *was* a holiday, and I could tell she'd popped too many pills already and now lingered in that strange wilderness that was semi-consciousness.

"It sure makes you think about God's blessings, don't it?" Her voice was a half-hum. "All of us here together. Praise God."

"Goddamn it. We forgot to say grace," Daddy said. "Wake up, Denise. I said *wake up*, dopehead."

He kicked her foot, her plate jostling in her lap as she inhaled sharply and sat up a little.

"Odette, you say it."

It had been like that since I was teenager. Daddy always made me say the family prayer, ever since I came home with that short haircut, as if he were secretly trying to make a point. For the first time ever, I did not refuse.

104

Odie

"BOW YOUR HEADS, then. Close your eyes."

I let my roll drop into my baked beans, setting my paper plate atop my knee. Daddy seemed taken aback by my lack of resistance. Bub did as I asked, but Denise was already asleep, her chin tucked down and eyes closed as if in prayer. Daddy did not close his eyes, watching me instead as he took his seat again in the recliner.

"Go on then," he said. "I'm listening."

"Dear Lord, thank you for this meal and this opportunity for us to be together today," I began, pressing my palms together under my chin piously. "Thank you for sending Bubba home to us for Christmas, and for all your help on his healing journey. I pray forgiveness for those who've wronged us, that you'll show them the same mercy and grace you've shown us, O Lord.

We want to pray for the meek, Lord, and the homeless, and those who don't have what we have this Christmas, and for all the little children who don't know you, Lord, please save them and grant them mercy. Lord, we want to lift up our neighbors, like Mr. Ennis Tulley, who keeps feedin' those community cats and letting 'em all die from inbreeding and disease. I wanna pray for the possums and raccoons, Lord, that Daddy will quit shootin' 'em, and that whore across the street, that Daddy will quit layin' with her."

Air rushed past my cheek, and I heard a pop like a firecracker, a bitter spray spitting across my face and plate. I opened my eyes, beer dripping down my forehead and cheeks from the bristles of my shaved head. Daddy had thrown a beer can at me, and it was skipping across the floor like a jumping bean.

Odie

"AMEN," I said, leveling my gaze at Daddy.

"Amen," Daddy said, opening a new beer and taking a long, hearty swig. "Clean that up, and get the pie out the oven, Odette. That's what I been waitin' on. Surely your dense little brain can handle that, since you want to be a smart ass today."

"Oh, yes, Daddy, I'm sure it can."

Denise's head had dropped back against the back of the sofa, her mouth hanging wide open, snores blaring from the back of her throat like the horn from an oncoming train.

A Christmas Story warbled on as I stood, picked up the beer can, and began the process of sopping up all the liquid.

Then there was the pie.

The pie lattice top had caramelized, the innards poking through and licking at the pastry as I pulled it from the oven to let it set. I dipped my finger into a diamond corner of the lattice, putting the hot drip of filling into my mouth and sucking. It tasted sweet and tart, and my jaw tightened like a drawstring. I'd never cared for cherry pie, but it was Daddy's favorite.

I couldn't wait any longer for it to cool, the buzzing in my belly was so strong. I cut one heaping piece of cherry pie for Daddy, topping it with a sloppy dollop of vanilla ice cream. The filling leaked across the plate like blood, the ice cream melting like a wax candle.

I carried the pie into the living room and set it on Daddy's lap, handing him a fork.

"Try it, Daddy. Let me know what you think."

He eyed me up and down, then sat up, scraping at the chunky round cherries with the edge of the fork, swirling them around in the melting ice cream. He got a bit of crust, cherry, and ice cream on his fork and took a large bite, stretching his mouth wide open to receive it.

I watched him chew and chew, the red filling seeping through his teeth, the cherries popping like blisters in his mouth.

"How's it taste, Daddy? It's my first time making it like this."

Daddy swallowed, washing down the sweet with the bitter beer, then taking another bite.

"It's good, Odie," he said, swollen cheeks full, the red of the cherry going straight to his eyes. "It's real good. What the hell did you put in this to make it so good?"

Odie smiled.

"Just cherries, Daddy. I wanted to make you something special."

Daddy scraped at the plate with his fork, scraped and shoveled the pie as if someone was gonna steal it out from under him. He looked up at me, spittle hanging from his lips.

"Might as well bring me the whole damn thing, I'm just gonna sit here and eat it all."

Odie

DADDY ATE from the pie dish with his bare hands, the filling dripping from his fingers and running trails down his arms. Spattered pieces were embedded in the thicket of his beard.

He scraped the plate clean, then licked at it, his green eyes rolling back in his head. He dropped to his hands and knees from the recliner, his hanging gut heaving once, twice.

A spray of cherries and blood splattered across the flat-screen TV, right across Ralphie's face in *A Christmas Story*.

"You alright, Daddy?" I asked, stepping back to avoid the spray, standing next to Bubba, wide-eyed in his wheelchair.

Bubba opened his mouth to speak, but only a rasp of a whisper came out, his breath a tremble.

Daddy reared up on his knees, grabbing at his

throat, making a thick choking sound. He heaved again, another spray erupting, painting the sleeping Denise's face, trickling into her open, snoring mouth.

A small, squirming thing lay in the bloodied vomit saturating the carpet, and Daddy clamored away from it, his hands shaking violently as if he was going through DTs.

I walked over to the flood of blood, dark as roadkill smeared across a lonely highway. I knelt down and picked up the thrashing newborn, smiling softly.

"Look, Daddy," I said. "Look what you've made."

EPILOGUE

ODIE PUSHED Bubba's wheelchair out the screen door, rolling it over the rough gravel patch masquerading as a driveway. She stood by the mailbox, beside the bull skull hanging on a rusty nail, taking in a deep breath of the crisp air.

"That was weird, wasn't it, Bubba?" she asked playfully, ruffling his light hair. "Don't worry, you won't have to see nothing like that no more. He birthed it, he can live with it now. Maybe it'll learn him a thing or two."

"You changed since you went to college," Bubba said softly, his hand on his throat. He could barely speak. He couldn't scream.

Odie's little hatchback was coming toward them in the distance, kicking up dust as it rocked down the gravel road.

"Yeah, I changed a little bit," she said. "But I changed more since I been home."

The car pulled up beside them, and Dale stepped out

of the car, a tall beanie sitting atop her bald head, her little pale ears like an elf's.

"Your chariot has arrived, My Darling," she said, kissing Odie deeply, a thin hand squeezing Odie's ass. Then she crouched and kissed Bubba on the cheek. "You coming with, Bubba?"

There were already duffle bags in the car, tents and wrapped sleeping bags, blankets and pillows, and a clattering cardboard case of moonshine lined up in crystalline mason jars like offerings to the gods.

Odie opened the back door, leaning on it. Sticky blood and cherry juice stained her hands, left a smear on the door handle.

"You don't have to come if you don't want to, Bubba. You can stay here, but I sure would miss you."

Bubba looked at Dale, then at Odie. Then he nodded, reaching for his sister to help him into the car. He could stand, but his legs felt weak. Dale moved to the other side of him, supporting his other arm as he was lowered gingerly to his seat.

Dale packed the wheelchair away, then climbed into the driver's seat next to Odie.

"Steatbelt, Bub," Odie said as she fastened hers.

The car's ignition screeched like a bat, then rumbled to life. Odie leaned over and kissed Dale again, then off they went, slipping and sliding atop the gravel as if they were in a race car, flying down the road and out toward the highway in a dirt plume.

Bubba's head rested against the cold glass of the window, his eyes watching the gray sky overhead.

He saw a flash of light color the clouds, quick as a

lightning strike, but much bigger and brighter than any he'd ever seen before. A spinning, spherical light appeared from the mist like a giant disco ball, lowering above the planet and painting the Arkansas plains silvery white.

Odie shifted forward in her seat to turn up the volume on the radio.

ACKNOWLEDGMENTS

Thank you first and foremost to the Kickstarter backers who made this project possible. Thank you for always believing in me, even when life got in the way. Through illness, surgeries, and losing a loved one, I felt y'all with me every step of the way. I'd like to extend a special thank you to Jamie Flanagan and Phil Nobile Jr., who both helped raise awareness for this project, and the following backers: Mike Flanagan, Barbara Crampton, Eric LaRocca, Gretchen Filker-Martin, Josh Malerman, Brea Grant, Hailey Piper, Victor Quinaz, Jeff VanderMeer, Kat Lockhart, Sarah Lopez, Jared Goode, Nor Never, Moksha Shah, Grey Low, Megan Kiekel Anderson, Patrick Maloney, James-Michael Fleites, Isabel J. Wallace, Lydia Joy, Leslie Kilgannon, Ryan Victor Czar, Bridget D. Brave, and last but not least, my real-life Dale, Noelle Burley.

I must thank my writing workshop and close friends Emma E. Murray, Shelley Lavigne, Lor Gislason, and Katrina Carruth for their mental, emotional, and physical support throughout this writing process. I would not have had the fortitude to complete this project without their guidance.

Thank you to Sam Richard for his friendship, Eric Raglin for his support and editing prowess, and Alan

Lastufka for his cover wrap design. Thank you to Kristina Osborn for the paperback front cover design and Amber Claus for the special edition hardcover design. Thank you for making my design. dreams come true.

Thank you finally to my spouse Jim for his enduring patience and calming presence through a process I never anticipated would be so damn hard. Thank you to Grandma, who just missed it by a hair. Love y'all.

Made in the USA
Middletown, DE
17 November 2024